The Legend of Ogden Jenks

THE LEGEND OF OGDEN JENKS

Robert Emmitt

McNALLY & LOFTIN, PUBLISHERS / 1970

Printed in the United States of America
By Kimberly Press, Inc.
Goleta, California

For my parents

The Legend of Ogden Jenks

1

THE TWENTY-ODD YEARS THAT crossed that high
plateau country like successive summer storms, bringing the nineteenth century close to its final decade,
carried their appropriate legends with them, deposit-
ing only a select few. Most of them, pertinent and
perishable as weekly newspapers, passed away with the
years, and one of these was the story of Ogden Jenks.
Within a very few years after his death — about the
time, perhaps, that the Census Office with its new elec-
tric tabulating machines was declaring the frontier
officially closed — only a man here and there, looking
wishfully backward, could talk of Og Jenks. One
man, the first of Og's several partners, bright eyes and
keen memory outlasting his body, had this to say
of Og:

"He a man with no belongin', Og was. Me, a black
dot in the allwhite, like maybe a hunk of coal drop
off'n a load and layin' there in a field of just-fell snow
alone till time ain't no more — sure enough alone, but
all the time hearin' the rumble of that there load that
done lost me off'n it, a million more black ones bumpin', load bumpin' its way along somewheres through
this world. . . . But it ain't so with Og. He ain't drop
off'n no load, cause they's no load of him — ain't even

3

one chunk like him no place. I listen and I got the rumble of that load in my ears; he listen (and I seen him many's the time, listenin' and listenin') but he don't hear nothin'. He just one chunk layin', don't matter where, from beginnin' to end. And most of all that chunk name of Og knowin' well enough that this is so — most of the time don't pine for no change of it. . . . But they's this one little bit of him reach out sometime like a birthed-blind baby — gotta touch the world and see for sure it's all warm. That there reach-in' — some might say it's the speck of good in the man; but I know, and I say that one speck of good is what done made the man all bad."

That was the summing up of Og's first partner, Dot, the runaway slave. Something of a summing up might also have been obtained from Og's final partner (for the first and the final partners were the only ones with the reckless patience to win — or to keep from losing), but the whereabouts of the final partner had not been known for many years.

The story of Og Jenks properly begins with the taking on of Dot as a partner — the gestation, the first reachings of the questing that Dot described. But his legend had earlier beginnings. For some it began with the changing of Og's face, for whatever face Og had come by naturally was a mistake and had to be remade after Og's way.

Looking backward still further, beyond the remade face, the figure and person of Og Jenks dims. The Stage Line officials, in their new and random-furnished outpost office, first saw a young man, a sullen and scrawny-necked oddity, loose-fitted and with narrow shoulders, hands hanging hugely out of blue-flannel sleeves — young in numbering of years; substance reading little of the print of years. If the face was later forgotten in its remaking, the mumbling metal of the voice was not — particularly the odd request that it made with few words, the first pressing of the legend of Ogden Jenks: he asked, very nearly demanded, that he be given charge of a station far from all settlement or talk of settlement — if possible, far from the casual travel, other than that of the coaches: some desolate and treacherous post that the Stage Line could only fill by desperate urging, threats, promises, and hazard pay. Og asked no favors; the Stage Line people complied with delight.

In those restless years between the extremes of wilderness and settlement, bands of renegade Indians often roamed petulantly away from their reservations. Usually, foxlike, they only nipped at the Stage Line's properties; but sometimes they openly terrorized, burned, and slaughtered. White men scattered thinly over that country before the coming of the range cattle were worse; and here, over the earlier years, Og Jenks was agent at several of the more remote stations — located reluctantly in some gloomy canyon or on a windy sage flat, perhaps justified by a spring or creek crossing and the usual pale green film of cottonwoods and willows and the accident of situation — a spot marking the limit of run for a span of horses and endurance of lady passengers bouncing in the badly hung coaches. But if any of Og's posts was ever molested there were no reports, no records — no written word from which to trace the growth of the epic that nonetheless grew.

The fable of Ogden Jenks — the spores of it blew in from the log, sod, and dobie buildings, the unpeeled pole corrals; the separation of man from flesh and will by force of talk and tale as the man, Og Jenks, had separated himself from the talk and its makers. In time, through no intent of his own, Og achieved a perverse immortality, birthless rather than deathless:

5

born into that wilderness without benefit of mother, coming into being there, at a time that no written language could record. . . . His knife, too — Og Jenks was not really alone. Was it a common ordinary knife? to look at, yes; but it was Og Jenks's knife. He scorned a gun as a form of human company but he carried the knife as though grown to him — a long, slim blade with a wrapped handle, in a scabbard fastened to his shirt pocket.

In his hands, Og's knife was a versatile tool, an adequate weapon: he could whittle and carve; he could slice, skin, gouge, chisel, pry, and hammer; he could slash and claw like a big cat, thrust like a white-gloved swordsman, send it through the air with the drive of a bullet and streak the hair from a head.

One line station had been plundered three times by white men then burned by Indians within six months. They assigned Og to it. With one word he sent away the helpers the company gave him and rebuilt the entire station. The drivers marked the progress of the work, step by step, as the coaches made their regular stops, until every log, corral pole, and roof shingle was in place; yet none of them ever saw Og at work. Some said the Indians came back, the white outlaws — all talk, with no trace of proof. The station stood unharmed through all the months Og stayed on the post.

When a coach pulled into one of Og's stations he would quickly and quietly hitch the fresh horses and run the spent ones into a corral for grain and water while the passengers went their brief ways to the slender sheds. Og would vanish, leaving the meager facilities of the station to the passengers and drivers to straighten bent muscles, slump on crude benches, or drink from the freshly filled water bucket. The stops were brief. Needs satisfied, all would collect and rattle

6

off behind the fresh span, leaving Og to the lonely peace he had chosen.

One afternoon a coach pulled into the station and Og was not there. Calling voices rang hollow among the buildings. Thoughts turned to outlaws, to Indians. But the horses milled hungrily, untouched, in the corral. The station's cashbox was in its place, unopened. The small store of food was intact. After a little talk, an exchange of bad guesses, drivers and passengers could only look at one another and say nothing. They all knew, or knew of, Og.

But talk there was, and by the end of the second day the intriguing mystery had spread over the miles. The second day another coach pulled in and another driver, more passengers made the search, called, and guessed. And the driver finally did as the one the day before had done — switched horses, left the spent ones behind with hay, grain, and water put out, and whipped his span on to carry the continued story down the road. On the third day the company sent out a party to search for Og and, if they found nothing, to bring in the extra horses and valuables before they went to thieves by default and to lock and board up the station. Certainly, they could find nobody to take it over now.

Og Jenks had just vanished. Nothing, not a trace. He had run away; something had frightened him off. Something? Something too big to even imagine, to scare Og Jenks. No, Og Jenks would never run. He would die in his tracks, if there were such a thing as could make him. And why even bother to unlock the cashbox and count the money? Og Jenks was no thief. Not that he was a good man — or a bad one either. Thieving was too much like something other people might do for Og Jenks to do it. The company prepared to write off Og Jenks and begin worrying —

worrying for nothing, because nobody, nobody within a thousand miles was going to take over the stage station from which Og Jenks had just disappeared into thin air.

Coaches, now making the double run with one span, took to flashing, all eyes forward, past the cluster of gaunt buildings gathered in the thin shade. A driver, perhaps a passenger, would venture a glance and swear he had seen out of the bouncing window a shape moving among the buildings, and the shape would sharpen in talk as the miles piled up. One driver, a brave man, saw it and pulled in his team, got down and searched, the inside rooms now thickening with dust where a trace of life would show plainly. If seeing something had stirred no fear in him, finding nothing did. He climbed on the box and whipped the horses into a run.

Days were long. It seemed months, but only ten days passed — a generation, in that country of few seasons. A stage climbed out of the shallow dip in the creek bend, and the driver, the shotgun rider, and four passengers all saw it — a figure squatting at the end of the cabin, hands busy. It was no shape that faded or flitted, but solid: the shape of Og Jenks, as the shotgun rider remarked, relaxing his nervous grip on his piece. Yes, the driver recognized him too, beyond a doubt. Og squatted there on the ground stretching a huge grizzly hide over a frame of aspen saplings.

Og, intent on his work, did not seem to have heard the coach pulling in. He did not turn nor straighten up when the driver, pulling to a halt beside him, called his name.

Then he did look up. He looked squarely at them, and the two toughened men up on the box turned quickly away.

Og stood up and, facing the coach with no face, walked forward. No face: the front surface of his head was a single swipe of a bear's paw, crimsoned and glossy with new scar tissue, flashing diagonally downward in an instant of violent motion. The eyes remained, generally in their places, still seeing but no longer a matched brace of organs. One was a slit with a living glint behind; the other was pasted wide, round, forever staring startled, socket drawn in a fiery crescent.

Og came and stood beside the coach, head tilted upward. Then he began to talk. The mouth, stretched long and tight and following powerfully the bear's oblique downstroke, moved with an animation of its own, while the ripped-down cheek bubbled air with each possible word. The driver tried to make his own mouth work, tried to form a word. But he could only crack his whip and send the coach hurtling on down the road.

At the far end of the run the Stage Line officials listened to what the driver, still somewhat tonguetied, had to say. Before sundown the company sent out riders to see to whatever needs Og might have. There were none, Og told them plainly, forming words in the formless face and at one devilish point nearly forming the least probable expression — a grin. He wanted only some change horses and supplies and to keep his post as always, without company. The rescue party was hungry and stayed for supper. Og proved that he had already taught his new face to eat and to smoke a pipe. The party decided not to stay overnight. They mounted their still-saddled horses, bedrolls in place behind cantles, and took the road toward headquarters in the gathering darkness.

After that the coaches continued to make their stops as before. The legend was whole, the face was its new core — a face of words, for few ever looked. Those who did so, inspired by the words, were compelled — the whole-featured, uniform events, identical ripples in the deep-flowing comfort; compelled by the truth that the deformed are the greatest events, the distinguished breaks in time — a look, then move back into the comfort of order.

"The ugly one down the way," they called him, or just "The ugly one." Og wore the name in proud silence, almost smugness, and in return received their silent respect.

And the records, which have no part of legends, showed that Og continued to serve the Stage Line for three more years, plus three months and eight days. Then early one spring he quit the line.

2

HE SENT WORD DOWN THE ROAD with the driver, along with a key and a bag of silver coin — fair enough price, they agreed, for the two horses he said he was taking with him. Still, the Stage Line people hoped it wasn't so. They questioned the next driver through, who reported that the station was locked up, everything cleaned up and in order — nothing gone except Og, his bedroll, his few possessions, and the two horses he had duly purchased. A week or two later word went around that a hide-hunter had sighted the ugly one, no mistaking it, riding and leading a packhorse that looked to be loaded with digging tools, headed off south toward the breaks and the canyons.

There seemed little doubt that Og had left. Little by little the company officials gave up their disbelief, telling one another less often that Og had, after all, disappeared for a long time to allow his new face to set. The thought kept the really troublesome matter back for the time being, but eventually they had to start talking about it: How were they ever going to get somebody to take over Og's station? The books were closed on Og Jenks.

Og had quit them suddenly, impulsively, the way men of strange ways do things. Even had they cared,

11

they could not have known the long deliberation that led to Og's leaving; known the day, leaning toward evening; the way Og sat staring through the greening curtain of willows into the spring-clear air across the sage flat and off to the massive swimming buttes on the horizon. How that scene had shrunk, those horizons drawn in over the shifting seasons and the unseen world beyond expanded to infinity.

They could not have known the thoughtful tapping, Og knocking out his pipe in the end, getting to his feet then hesitating as though fearing in the moment whatever it was possible for him to fear, walking with a determination, boldly back inside to his tangled bed, where he stooped and dragged out the tin box.

The unearthing of the box from its place under the bed was a quiet ritual that followed the early supper, the pipe, and the staring time on the wooden bench under the unpeeled supports of the long porch; but this day Og moved as though cutting the head off a chicken. Open a lid, peer inside as usual — but today with the jerky motions that put aside finality. He put the box back. He would go away now and leave it, go back to his continuing perusal on the porch. But not today. Almost the instant he replaced the box and sat upright, he bent double and hauled it back out. He opened the lid again (the box had never been locked; it had never been that far from Og, except once) and counted the money. His hands slowed, their quick movements smoothed, he recounted the money, on and on into the sweet spring dusk with its chill softly entering the open door.

When the next coach pulled in, Og changed the horses as always. When the coach pulled out, the driver held in his head the words of Og's quitting and in his hand a small bag of silver.

Og took the trail south, just as the hide-hunter had reported — indeed, as Og had always planned — into the country that no man would try to claim for his own for many years to come, that no man would ever really succeed in claiming, although it would break many and kill others who tried; wild, impulsive country where even the scant trails of wildlife were tenuous, washed out seasonally by flash floods that left the thin soil worn to expose bare bedrock and to bake to a glaze in the dry months and powder to ash underfoot.

Days melted together under the strengthening sun and drew out to flashing dawn-and-dusk intervals marking the changing moons. Og prospected for minerals. He panned the scant streams and dug test pits (somewhere he had seen or heard tell of it being done); he attacked the rock with a pick and when the handle snapped he fashioned another with his knife out of a seasoned sapling, chosen, felled, and neatly laid out by some long-gone beaver that had already spent its measure of energy. Through the months his undirected ways covered a wide expanse of country, up the gray-brown desert and into the low hills; to the higher slopes where the first pines stood shamelessly above the juniper, scruboak, and piñon; down into the breaks and up the river with its feeding streams. With a loud laugh he swung his pick at mocking walls of rock, gouging their faces and bringing down tons of boulders.

But something — a tightening loop — began to draw around him, and in the early fall he noticed that his range had slowly narrowed and, finally, that he had been keeping a permanent camp for many days. He noticed it with the throe of a man marking his years; his actions, always for themselves alone, had become infected with something like a purpose, demanding to be identified. His interest, diffused over that country-side poor even in unliving mineral, had turned inward upon what appeared to be a thin scattering of lead carbonate with possible traces of silver.

His camp and his diggings were located in a low, wide canyon a mile or two above the junction of a fast-splashing creek and the slow, laboring river. A clear spring flowed from the base of the rocks near his camp, and the canyon floor itself was a jungle of cottonwood, sycamore, alder and willow, all roped with vines. The lip of the canyon was fringed with stout pines.

The spring formed a clear pool before it trickled into the creek, and just below the pool was the apparent location of what Og took to be the lowgrade ore he had begun hoarding as he had once hoarded coin in his tin box. This spot, like a checkerboard between pondering players, had become all creation.

Each evening Og squatted and raked together his growing pile of rocks, weighed it bit by bit in his cupped hands and sifted the finer stuff between his fingers; the larger chunks he turned round and round to catch the light of the sunset, which never quite caught on the dull surfaces. Often at night, weak with sleeplessness, he would creep out of his bedroll, as though someone nearby might discover his actions, and examine the pile under a good moon. It was his, that was the important thing. He had found it. It was lowgrade stuff; even Og with his scant knowledge of minerals could see that. It was lowgrade and not enough to make mining pay. It was his; it demanded nothing of him. He demanded nothing but to look at it in the evenings, at night under the moon when he couldn't sleep.

Days wore and the pale traces of silver faded. One clear, cool evening they vanished with the colors in the sky and did not return with the sun. Og cursed.

He bored into the drab hillside with his crude tools and cursed aloud into the ringing daylight of the canyon. He brought down more rocks, more and more, huge ones and tiny ones, smashing the huge ones to bits like a man newly awake trying to drag back a dream. He examined samples under the sun then hurled them with a weak crash down among the tangled trees in the creek bottom. He threw the broken little nodes of rock away one by one, and because he was looking for the black thread of silver in the lusterless leaden stone he threw away many before he really looked — looked and saw that the color had been changing in front of his eyes. Looked at the bright bluegreen of copper. He had hit a seam of highest grade copper ore.

Og dropped the sky-colored ore and squatted over it, settled back on his hams and passively let the large fact of discovery course through him. It left him befuddled, and the second time he was beset by the new knowledge, it left him a trifle unhappy. Unhappy, because the search was ended. He had saved and planned for many years for the search. He had never really thought about the find. The search had given him brief pleasure and had come to a tedious end. He picked up the rock and closed his fist over it until the veins swelled in his forearm. Thoughts needled him — assays and claim-filing, yellow legal paper in chalk-dry offices, disposal of ore to custom smelters and market prices printed fine in week-old newspapers out of the East.

But he knew he would stay in this place, dig out the ore and sell it; money would again pile in his little tin box. At the moment, he could think of nothing else to do, and he doubted that he would ever think of anything else.

He could quit swinging his pick at rock for a while and start swinging his ax at trees. There would be new days filled with another doing — something birthing and building; and after a dark sleep in his bedroll he plunged into the new days and trees fell; then he polished his ax blade with his sharpening stone, felt it with his thumb and more trees fell, branches skinned off and notched logs grew into their places and walls lifted out of the ground.

The site, more happening than choice, pleased Og. A few steps from the gap between the placed logs that would bcome a door, a bucket could be dropped into the spring that had just survived the driest of seasons; from the site on the slope above the rockledge brow of the spring he could view the canyon from wall to wall to its mouth and through to a wide piece of the valley and the river glinting in the sun on the flat roughed with flourishing brush, on to the wall of pink and yellow stacked in a bluff across the valley, perhaps twenty miles away — bright silent miles where sign of intrusion could be felt before seen.

For many days the work seizure held him. He arose in the morning, often forgetting to eat, and attacked the day and time dripped on into dusk. He forgot the ore and all its possible meanings in the flurry of his new work. His mind, muscled and vacant, shut it out. But in time the work began to fag. It slowed and came to a halt at the time for putting on the roof, and the four windowed walls stood empty and open to the sky, with Og sitting staring idly through the hours at the ragged green grass on the floor. He tried, pushed; his will had become a rock that outweighed him, the work had cooled like a fever out of his hands and arms and back. He wandered peevishly through the days, kicking rocks and trees, slashing the air with his knife or throwing it, sometimes to lance into a tough old tree, other times to pin a small running animal squealing to the ground.

He tried to turn back and burrow deep into the shallow tunnel, pry at the ore seam, the rich color — rich; he could not fit himself to it or, as he turned back, to the walls of the cabin awaiting a roof, a door; nothing to watch, to see except the sunset and it came, the dark. He sat on the grass late into the night and other nights with the stars wheeling slowly around the pivot of his oversize fire, burning prodigiously the wood he had pressed himself out of the bedroll to rustle that morning. He was getting up later each day and sitting on his spread bedroll before he could get himself to gnaw stomachless at the sinking stock of food. Later in the day he would pin a cottontail with his knife, then toss the carcass off for the coyotes to feed in the moonlight. Skinning and drawing — small, tedious task, too small, just as other tasks were too large. Night would make its wearisome return and he would rouse himself to carry armloads of wood to his fire-building.

Deep into the night, wood gone, fire dying, he would slide into his bedroll and wait for sleep. He would know that it had finally slipped up on him in a later instant of sitting stark upright, chest pounding him toward getting into his clothes; coach due in a little before dawn, horses to feed and water, corral to clean, more horses to tend for the southbound stage in the afternoon. A bit of dark time, and he knew it was long to dawn and finally to know that no stage was coming in today — no stage in all his years, in this country that was all around him for many silent miles. A dream . . . not exactly; more, being picked up bodily and set back over months in one fool instant quickly broken by a desolate wind up the canyon out of the cooling valley. He would sink back on his blankets

17

and tarps to stare at the stars through the eye that wouldn't close. Next time, perhaps, sleep would stay the night.

One night when he started awake that way, long after the moon was down and the black sky was spirited with dawn, he lay and listened to the voices of the creek, the canyon crowded with marching, rushing, words dropping out of the water's many voices and falling. He lay until he was sure he had to get up; then the voices vanished and the common sound of downslanted water replaced them. He built a fire and watched day form on the rim while he boiled water for coffee. In a better light he caught his horses, packed one and saddled the other.

Once through the gate of the canyon he took the trail up the river and out of the valley, to the high desert where a wagon road climbed the folds of land toward cooler greener country, toward town. Daylight swelled full. . . . Needed tools, dynamite, claim filings, assays, and his name scratched in a column in a big bound book. Pattering thoughts and the night was behind.

3

THE ROAD STRETCHED straight, waving in the warmth
of the early autumn noon. Far out ahead Og sighted
a man on horseback.

Og would hang back, keep to himself. Slowed as he
was by a packhorse, he probably would not catch up
even if he tried. The horseman was a good mile off,
raising a fair dust cloud that told he was moving along
at a good gait. Yet before long Og saw clearly that he
was gaining on the other rider. He pulled in his horse
and his thoughts wandered ahead to his duties in
town. Soon he saw that again he was gaining. He
stopped his horses — for a rest, he told himself, and
to justify it he traced with his fingers the sweat patches
forming below the withers. But he had to push on,
and in time he noticed that again the space between
him and the other rider was shrinking. It was just
about calling distance now, and before Og could think
of what next to do, call was just what the other traveler
did. He turned in his saddle and called back a greeting, which Og did not return. But he could do nothing
but let himself catch up to the turned and grinning
face — a face unsuited in its own fashion to the world
as was Og's. Og fell in beside the horse, which turned

19

out to be a mule plodding indifferently, head low and ears lopping — the mule, the reason Og had not been able to keep distance and travel alone.

The face was black. It belonged to a man named Dot, with no other ready identity except "runaway slave," which was too much and hardly enough. The War between the States was half a decade gone and the word *slave* was a state of mind. It did not fit this man Dot; a slave had to have a master — a man, time, the elements, or the creation of his own mind. Certainly, as this man Dot was known and known widely, he had never had any real sort of a master. And the other word, "runaway," was not right either. Running away? No; walking away perhaps, in the careless plodding manner of the mule he now rode.

He was an ageless Negro, short and slow and strong with skin black to a high gloss; and the effort of creating the present pink and white grin pumped out the meandering veins at his temples.

"You's goin' to town too so we'd as well be company; no sense you ridin' back a piece like that."

Og made no reply — but then Dot had not asked a question; merely observed something that could not reasonably be denied, giving his mule a backward kick with bulging laced shoes to pace him with Og's horse, then taking no issue with Og's silence.

After a mile or so, side by side, Dot did ask a question.

"You been out prospectin'?"

But even the question was a flat statement, something like a challenge, designed to get an answer.

Og had to say, "Yuh."

"Find any gold?"

"Nope."

They were the first words the two men had ever exchanged in the years of knowing each other by hearsay — the invisible tags by which men were recognized in such chance meeting: Og the mean ugly one who kept to himself and had once killed a grizzly with only his knife and had lost his face; Dot, the runaway slave who had never run from anything, who lived nowhere but always seemed to live, and relatively well, wearing his black face with a maddening dignity.

The Dot of hearsay now, riding beside the talked-of Og Jenks, pushed his hat backward on his head (a good fur felt that could easily have cost him or somebody fifteen or twenty dollars) and wiped his glossy forehead with a stained bandanna.

"Guess maybe you givin' her all up then."

Another calculated observation that slipped past Og's wariness and drew words.

"Why should I?"

And Og began to wonder, Why did he find himself riding toward town beside this black man when he had done everything he could to prevent it, short of turning around and riding the other way? He could not remember fully, but he seemed to recall that this nigger was always about half wanted by whatever law there happened to be, but never quite enough to make it worth any lawman's while to arrest him. Nobody quite liked him, but nobody disliked him enough to do away with him. His name seemed vaguely linked to every outlaw bunch in two territories, yet he had the feel of a loner. If he had a mean streak Og did not know it, nor did he sense it now — and this aspect of a man's character was something every person fitted for survival in that time and place learned to sense. Only a few hard pebbles sifted out: Dot was a man who rarely worked for wages, owned nothing productive, yet always seemed to find the means to get along — with a touch of luxury here and there.

And Og — Og was not the same now, no longer the

21

keeper of a remote stage outpost. He had gone out looking and now he owned (he tried again to fit himself to it but couldn't, quite) something somebody else would want.

"So I's just guessin'. I's guessin' you givin' her all up and goin' back to town. That's the first guess come to me, mind you; but then you ask me, Why should I? Meanin', I guess again, why should you give her all up? Then I see here you is goin' to town just like I said, only you say why should you give her all up; that make me think maybe you got somethin' you might could give up, only you say you ain't found nothin'."

Og took his pipe from his pocket and scraped the last crumb of tobacco from his worn elkhide pouch, thinking how he would be able to show this asking nigger an empty pouch when he tried to beg some tobacco; but when the tobacco was finally tamped and the pipe shoved into the upper corner of Og's mouth, Dot was leaning out of his scuffed McClellan saddle, three sulphur matches in his horny black paw. Og could do nothing but snatch the matches from the hand and try to use one of them. A breeze was ruffling the brown, warted, and slowturning countryside, and Og had to use the second match and then, to his chagrin, the third. Dot never quit talking.

"Now you say, Why should I? and I ain't sayin' you should; but first I hear you say, nope, you ain't found nothin'; then you, ridin' along here beside me on your way to town (cause they ain't noplace else this road go, less'n you got business with some prairie dogs along the way), you say why should you give it all up and go back to town. That's all I mean, mind you: you ain't found nothin' and you ain't givin' it up nohow."

"That's because you ask me did I find any gold."

Og's sprung jaw clamped down on the pipe. The talk had been nibbling away at him, and he had known that he would either have to say something or take his knife and cut the wind off that fed the words. But he wished he had not said that. The nigger seemed all too pleased with what he had finally drawn out of Og's mouth.

Og added, "Best you don't be askin' nothin' at all and best you quit guessin'."

It was enough: the remark together with the Og Jenks of hearsay silenced Dot. And silence was better fitted to the rising heat and dust and the climbing road pointing toward the forward-creeping low range of mountains in the east. The grass gradually thickened, richened the slowly rising land and raised its million autumn heads, and the junipers lifted out of it taller and straighter, leaving their twisted forms below. The flat landscape folded and humped into hills; just ahead stood the first pines, neat as fence pickets. Beyond them, just out of sight, was the town.

The rising hills drew in on either side of the road, the breeze that had bent the grass now rushed briefly through the branches overhead for one last sigh, and the road became the main street.

Og felt the busy buildings line up as he kept his eyes to the brown space between, grass and natural cover barely worn away in the brief years of settlement; this, called street, was as deserted as its own countryside. The sounds of town? They were inside his own head, paced by thoughts: things to do, demands that had put him here: buying, bargaining, writing, recording, signing, faces facing, faced. Man and mule, plodding beside him, were shut out.

Dot had fallen in with Og's thinking aloud, the habit of two alone men shared for the moment.

"Sure you do," Og heard Dot saying, "sure you got a lot of doin' ahead of you, but a man wants to be busy in the doin' of it, not in the thinkin' of it. Thinkin'

23

don't tote no loads. A man's brains ain't the muscles to tote the loads he thinks up. Now lookie here: the sun's agoin' down and the time for doin' is when she come up again, bright and slept-out. In between, then's the time for restin', like you goes to bed and sleeps good but before that you has a drink or two. You goes in them doors over yonder and they's a piano bangin' in your ears and a lot of fool talk goin' on. You takes a little short drink." Dot measured with thumb and forefinger, squinting one eye to fit the space. "Then another little feller, maybe three, but not too many. Next thing that there piano you maybe wanted to take a ax to gets soundin' mighty sweet and the fool talk — maybe you wants to make a little of it yourself; ain't no real hurt in it. Then's really the time for sleep. You snuggles into that bed and closes your eyes on a real fine world — or we'll say that's the way she's lookin' to you by this time, and lookin'-like makes it so. The world's in your eyes, and when they close up on all this livin' ain't no more world than Judgment Day. If three, four whiskeys puts a fine world in my eyes, then I say they's the juice of heaven, worth a whole lot more'n the coin they takes from me. But they's one last whiskey that can make the world purely rotten. That there's the one I never takes."

Og had done very little drinking in his life. Drinking in a bar was for men who liked company; drinking alone was for men who wanted to like company and did not know how. But Dot's words pressed like a gentle weight at his back, and he was tying his horses to the rail beside the mule. He moved easily, mindlessly through the doors and into public.

Many had passed the tale that Og was a bad drunk. Violence had its large part in the Og Jenks of hearsay, his knife and the work of it — more in the telling than the doing. And where in the name of talk did violence live, except in a bottle? The scattering of men along the bar quietly withdrew; men older to the region furtively passed the word. Strangers watched with them, tales fortified by the sight of Og — watched eagerly for what was certainly going to happen to the black one.

Dot ordered and the bartender set out a bottle and two glasses, flipping frightened glances at Og, then retreated to the now-crowded opposite end to talk, hand in front of mouth. Dot poured two drinks, held up his glass with a grin and drank. The whiskey leaped up in Og's stomach like a warm body.

Dot slid the back of his hand across his mouth, studied Og, and smiled again.

"Now you ain't the only one. You see I got business in town too, like one of the finest five-string banjos in this big country over across the way in pawn. I been havin' a lean spell, and the leanest of it is I got to do without my music for nigh three months. I got to take what music comes my way, and for me it ain't nothin' beside what I make myself. Tomorrow's the day for gettin' out that there banjo. Tonight I already hears the music comin' out her, and it make me smile in my drink. No, ain't totin' no burdens tonight. Tomorrow I totes that banjo, and tonight I have the drinks and hear the music from her, hear it like I got her here in my arms thwanin' away at her." Dot talked on and Og split inside, half of him trying to understand why he was here at all and where in his time was this place, the other half spreading itself to the warmth creeping out of the drink in his stomach and listening with drifting interest to the words of the man he had met on the road. Dot poured another drink for each of them and talked on, "Then here's another drink and prob'ly after bit we have us another, but that goin' be where she stop for me; I got a good night to sleep, but first

I got me a girl to set with. She's a greaser that like to fool around with me the way I like to be fooled around with by a girl, and for me too much whiskey got no part in that. Just enough to skin the ice off the bucket, then I be leavin' out of here and I be sayin' goodbye and nice ridin' with you and buyin' you a drink," and he studied Og's face briefly, "less you got a mind for the foolin'-around kind of girls. This here greaser one I tell you about got a sister likely feels a good bit the same way. We could have us one more drink and go a-visitin'."

Og reached for the bottle and poured. Dot held out his glass and grinned into the brown fluid, his lips drawn back and a tune humming long and deep and sweeping as a hymn between his teeth. He drank and put words to the tune:

> Lottie she's a gal in red,
> Dressed in sin from feets to head;
> But when I get that dress off'n her,
> She so sweet and she so pure,
> I dress her all up in one kiss . . . mmmmmmo . . .

Dot made more music through his lips and teeth, seeding in words more and more heavily until the song broke over into talk: "I spect you never hear that there song before, no, you don't never hear it because I make that one myself long time ago and I don't recollect I ever done sung it once, twice after I get her made. Ain't me make it; it's that old banjo I talk about done made it, make all my songs. Ain't made none in nigh three months."

Dot's talk continued hardly distinguishable from song — misfit music in the uncommonly silent gloom of that public room, gloom entering the door off the street and out of the sky; for in the opening which might soon let in half the town daylight had vanished and the hanging lamps with their flaring cone shades deep in the room were lit, inviting the gathering at tables. The bartender drew down the lamp over the bar and lit it, and it floated upward through stiff parchment of smoke from the bartender's broomhandle-sized cigar. The watchers far down the bar had shrunk as a group; those who remained had turned their attention from Og to Dot, no longer curious and less than disappointed; for storms were always making, few ever broke. Og had forgotten that there were others in the saloon and was staring huge-eyed at Dot.

"Sing something else."

Dot made his mouth into a lipped grin. "Not me, ain't singin' time. Right now I spect it's eatin' time, then girlin' time, or whatever time it want to be, I ain't choosin': time to plant and time to pluck up that which is planted. Prob'ly about now I'll be leavin' your company, cause that's the way time does me. I'll wish you best luck, minin' man — you lone minin' man," and he dug a balled fist into his pocket. He was going to leave then, leave Og in this place of gathering, the first of such places as his owning would put him. Weakly, Og reached into his own pocket and felt the coin. He brought it out. All silver, except for the three copper pennies, and he stared at the pennies. He laid one of them on the bar, and his unworkable mouth worked without thought.

"See there. Where you made your mistake was askin' me if I'd found gold. Right there's what I got, and pure enough ore to make a million of those without half refinin' it."

Dot slowly pulled his hand from deep in his lopping trousers and let it hang. He stared at the penny on the bar. Then his big purple lips again rolled back. "Man, coin is coin. You find gold and they make coin

27

of it, you find silver and they make more coin, and them's got the coin makes men work hard to get it. But copper; now who'd ever think twice of it — but that's coin too, and right there by your hand on the bar is shinin' proof of it; and it's a good bit more'n just coin. Gold, well she the white boss man's daughter, silver she his wife, but copper, that's the workin' folks. You hear tell of gold dishes but you don't never see none; you hear tell of a copper shell case and you see it and believe it. I done ask you if you found gold, and that's my fool thinkin'; like everyone else's fool thinkin' I think prospectin' and I think gold. But copper . . . "

Og studied the penny as it lay flat. He stood it on edge and admired it some more, then he spun it and let its perfect orb catch the lamplight. "Richest copper vein I reckon anybody ever seen in these parts."

Dot too watched the penny, draping his scuffed elbow over the bar out of a rolled sleeve; he inched closer to Og and held his voice reverently low. "I tell you right now what you need is a partner. You figure you find it and it's yours and you figure right. But the findin' is only the start of it all, and you beginnin' to see that now, here with all this townin' to do. They's assayin' and filin'. Then the world know and they watch and think, seein' for you to make some fool mistake; ain't sayin' you do, mind you, but they waitin' just the same, and they got all kinds of thinks on it, and if you ever go to figurin' who is *they,* you can figure it's all the rest of the world that don't want one man to keep what's his'n, and that one man is you. Then that ore's to be got out and sold to them that smelts it down, and that takes more savvy. Ain't sayin' you ain't got it, but two men with savvy's got a lot more of it than one; and me I been minin' here and there. Started off in California and worked east — Ne-

vada, Idaho, Montana. I seen gold, and the silver come
after, and the copper come last and make the most —
for the keepers, and they ain't usually the finders. And
somethin' else it takes is money. Like I said, I been
havin' a lean spell. But I just now come by a bit of
money — ne'mind how — and it's enough to get that
there banjo out pawn and some more. Enough to get
all the tools and such I'd ever need to work a mine,
only I ain't got no mine." He stood up straight then
and grinned off into the far end of the saloon room.
"No mine, so I got no call to be thinkin' such things,
do I? No, ain't minin' time. It's girlin' time and eatin'
time and timin' time, so I guess we say I buy these
drinks since you in here by my invitin', then I go on
my way."

But he didn't leave right then and Og had some
long and hectic thinking; and at last when Dot did
leave the saloon Og left with him and they took a dark
alley behind new brick buildings until the alley became a path beside a rushing creek where tall pines
hid the traces of town and the fringe of twilight over
the round and toothed hills; finally the path led to a
downcast shack with orange-lit windows where two
pretty Mexican girls lived with a blind father, a trio
far, strange, and accidental — isolated from desert
sun and miscast in northern autumn; and the girls
began the evening by wrapping mashed beans in huge
tortillas and serving them to Dot and Og with bright
giggling. But before Dot and Og left the saloon they
had poured still a fourth drink — to their partnership.

4

THE LARGEST AND LAST of their many purchases the
next day was a big spring wagon that would carry back
to the mine all they had bought and would return
with twice its weight in ore; to pull the wagon they
bought a team of heavy dray mules. These last, vet-
erans of railroad-building, caused the first unrest between Dot and Og. Dot had made all the selections in
tools and equipment, even in food supplies, for here
Dot insisted he was an expert cook who would "cook
the last supper for Jesus." Og didn't like mules, and
the worst of it was he couldn't say why.

"Mules," Dot pronounced the word as the title of a
lecture, "why man ain't nothin' for a mine but mules.
They go in a black hole couldn't turn around a rabbit
in and they come right out, right end up. They pull
anything cause they too cussed to admit they can't pull
it, and they ain't scared of nothin'. You don't like
mules? Well, hell, they don't like you neither, and
that make livin' with them all the easier. They don't
like nobody, even mostly other mules. They ain't
natural animals and they didn't make theirselves that
way. You gives a little somethin' to them and they
gives a little somethin' to you, just so's you leave them
be the rest of the time, and they more than ready to

leave you be. You got respect for them and they got respect for you; they ain't no likin' in it. Ain't nothin' for me but a mule."

Dot won and the partnership truly began, filled with equal parts of talk — Dot's talk — and of silence which was Og's. And from that moment Og's deep reluctant need for Dot grew — need all contrary to the being of Og. Dot thought hard and well and aloud and Og listened, for he had never learned to talk.

They loaded the wagon and Dot the kindred soul of mules took the reins, and they began the trip back to the mine with the saddle stock tied on behind the wagon, minus the horse Og had used for pack, which had been given in trade for the dray mules, so that Og's tired saddle horse was forced into the companionship of Dot's dirty roan mule. The ore had assayed unbelievably rich, the filing had taken a tortured hour in the land office and the purchasing had brought them into bright midday. Out of the town again the clean breathless country looked and felt good. The sun had long since met and overmatched the threat of frost, and now they were dipping downward where no frost would hit for perhaps another month and where the winter snow would never lie for more than a day. The mountain sky was ice blue and the brown road dust was hot. Meadowlarks and redwing blackbirds sang out and hopped the crests of the brush like large clean insects.

Out on the road Dot wrapped the reins and reached back for his banjo, all of him that there was in that wagon except for the oversized saddle rifle that lay behind the wagon box.

O Madeline I'm poor no more,
O Madeline I'll pass your door;
Now I got riches, I'll buy me diamond bitches.

O Madeline you got to find
That I just ain't your kind.

Og listened, dropped his head and dozed and
dreamed; for last night had been dark with no seeing
and he had been with a woman.

No money can buy me,
No jailhouse can hold me,
No woman can fool me;
I'll stay my own man.

Out to the right the sun slipping south fell, weakened and reddened. In the color of sunset Dot stopped
the wagon in a grove of willows, unharnessed mules,
untied horses and buckled on feed bags; Og dipped
water from the stream and Dot built a small cartwheel-
shaped fire and cooked. Then, rolled up in the faraway silence, each briefly remembering town, they
fell into copper riches and deep sleep.

Travel with the heavy wagon was slower than by
saddle, and beyond the end of the road bumped several miles of little-used trail touched by nothing more
civilized than the shod hoof of a grass-fed horse; there
were abrupt dips into coulees to break spokes or axles;
but Dot was, as he had promised, a skillful driver; the
mules worked with his will and the wagon crawled
through while Dot, his banjo finally laid aside, gave
full hand to the reins and haltingly composed a song
without benefit of fingers or strings about a wicked
woman-killing man on the trail to possible damnation,
which turned out in the end to be a spiritual corollary
of the gallows. Another sundown was beside them
when they ended the last and most primitive stretch
of trail up the steep canyon to Og's camp.

Dot dropped to the ground and humming and tapping his foot studied the unfinished cabin and the site while Og, still up on the wagon seat, watched. In spite of his prosaic posture the Negro's studying held an insinuation of criticism, perhaps disdain — as though, Og thought, he had just bought the place and was tediously planning to undo the bad actions of the last tenant; he even took in the ring of stones Og had rigged for a fireplace and the cottonwood trunk charged with protruding nails where Og hung his cooking gear. Slow rage that must go nowhere swelled in Og, but Dot just hummed.

"Got some big plans, have yuh?" Og asked. Dot only went on with his study, nodded without turning to Og, a grin in the shape of his cheeks. Finally he walked back to the wagon and began unhitching. "Come on, they's eatin' time and sleepin' time, and tomorrow's minin' time."

Next morning Dot rolled out with a song, built one of his own kind of fires and cooked a breakfast of salt side and sourdough cakes made from a jar of starter Og had carefully hoarded in a tiny cave under the cool spring and which Dot sniffed judgingly before mixing his dough. After a long drink from the bucket of powerful coffee, with the camp tidied up for the first time in many weeks and tidier than it had ever been at its best, Dot mumbled, making words fit the tune he had been fashioning since daybreak — words that now seemed to be shaping into a song about going and having a look at "our mine." He hoisted a dynamite crate on his shoulder and with a swing of his head drew Og in behind him with sledges and drills, and he took Og's beaten path that Dot seemed to have made with his own feet and led the way to what he might well have called "my mine."

He scrutinized the shallow, hand-dug tunnel, reboring it with his eye through the lowgrade silver ore streak and muscled rock shadowing and rippling into the vanishing black and promising body cavity of the hill, redoing each faulty stroke of pick and shovel with a song subdued to a lively whisper, toiling thought often drawing away sound and leaving lips to move silently; his manner was confident and assuring; he seemed to be making something of a covenant with some familiar in an ancient partnership that whatever had been done wrong would be redone right and that whatever was done in the future would be more than successful — that in the end some grand and secret objective would be achieved. The song then stalled in a depth of thought and resumed with a scattering of new words, evoking images of such as timbers to shore up and old devil dynamite to reach out for big proud mister copper vein — or the old bad live Indian under his hill that got to be made good with a big white man boom. He lit a lantern and advanced into the tunnel, scraped and shoveled and bent and scratched and stretched to peer at bare rock, run his finger along cracks and seams as though feeling for a pulsebeat. Then he came back out, pried the lid off the case of dynamite with the flattened end of a rock drill, spit on his hands and picked up a sledge and shook it at the mouth of the tunnel, which gave its evocative "O" back to his words: "I comin' to get you. Look out, Mister Richman Vein, I comin' in fury and rage to tear you right out that big old mansion house of yours, that big old rock house you think keep you so safe from all these niggers for leven million billion years." He cackled gloriously and strode into the tunnel; then he turned toward Og like a small boy reluctantly remembering his manners toward an elder who could only blunt the joys of the young. "Bring along the drill; Ole Richman got to lose his happy mansion house."

Og followed, his bickering feelings dulling his

brain: he knew at last his need, but he knew better his hatred for such need. Inside the tunnel Dot again studied and felt and scraped and finally tapped a spot with the end of the drill and motioned Og to take his place. Dot swung and the hammer rang and his song went up in the gloom and smell of violated earth and unsunned rock; Og's hands stung and he tightened and twisted. "I ain't goin' miss that drill and you ain't goin' let go it, mister partner man." Dot's muscles swelled spiritedly against the faded blue shirt which soon began to turn dark.

When he judged the hole deep enough, Dot stopped abruptly and packed it with dynamite, strung the fuse behind him as he crept in a squat toward daylight. Og followed. Dot lit the fuse and they crouched under the stream bank silently watching the smoking spark creep back toward the tunnel. Then the blast shot back at them and Dot's genial screech cut the heavy rolling voiceless echoes. They smashed, shoveled, graded, drilled, and blasted again before the day quit them.

At sundown a wind came up and blew in a vast sea of frozen air; then the stars came out in a clear sky, still and cold, and the partners crowded the meager warmth of the fire after squatting close with seared faces and stiffened backs to press food into their mouths. Dot limbered his fingers on the strings of the banjo. "We goin' be two rich men freezin' cold in a poor old shack pretty soon. We got to roof out that there cabin yonder, then where we be? No stove in there, we still got to come outside to do our cookin' and get warm and one chunk of ore like my two fists buy us the best stove in the hardware store. Guess maybe it's back to town and get us a little old stove for inside there where they's walls and a roof to keep in the warm stead of lettin' her go out to the trees and stars. Then I be cookin' on top a iron stove like a white man stead of on a old open campfire like a Indian, and we got us two warm bunks for beds and all. Tomorrow we got to blast some more, look into that deep ore pile and see what we got, then we take a few days and fix up our house and go to town and get us a stove and maybe visit them two greasers again."

It all got done just as Dot had sung it over his banjo. The next day they blasted again and Dot graded the ore and regraded it, handling the highgrade daintily in his big purple hands. Then, it seemed, with a few of Dot's puttering motions a respectable cabin was standing on the site, with a floor and a door hung on hinges of harness ends and two windows that would draw shut against weather. When it came time to go to town Og shook his head and hung behind and Dot drove the wagon out alone, singing out of sight.

For the days that Dot would be away would be for Og days of an older order, a life that was himself, for which he had begun to starve — for just a dribbling taste now, perhaps, that would stop his ears to Dot's untainted joy with almost everything, the tickling biting insect hovering over the surface of skin, laughing at inept swatting hands and stirring rage deep below. Dot's joy, his own contained and self-sufficient solitude that could persist in a crowd, his open display of mastery, of himself and therefore of all: and it was the mastery (no, it was Dot's money investment, Og kept trying to insist, then gave up), the mastery was the need, and the need the insect, the fly that would not be swatted. The mine was being mined, the cabin was built, and neither had gotten done while Og was alone here; these days of Dot's absence from the camp were not the true day, the other days of being alone, performing alone under the trusting, silent, and unseeing mastery of the Stage

Line, and now Dot had become the master by necessity and default. Og stood over the fire that night until the bottoms of his trousers smoked and he cursed up at the stars and yelled back at a sassy coyote. By day he stared into the blade of his knife which could have cut out almost anything except vacancy. On the fifth day when Dot's song sounded up the canyon the silence settled over Og, but far inside he was the eager running child, seeing at last the tipping wagon and the gleam of the new cast-iron stove.

The stove had curved legs with scrolls and leaves worked into the bright gray iron, and there were two lids in the oblong top and a small reservoir for hot water. Soon it was in place in the cabin corner with its pipe passing through the roof and sealed tightly with sheets of tin. Dot had also brought two ticks filled with straw and panes of glass cut and measured for the windows and a bucket of sorghum molasses for which he admitted he had paid three prices but had been craving for his sourdough cakes.

The stove was fired. Bunks were built of woven rope with the ticks flattened against their frames and the bedrolls unrolled for good, to be dignified as true beds. "Now we needs us a blizzard, though I don't spect we get more'n a pee-widdlin' one down here. Man don't know he got him a home till come along a good piece of weather and wind rattles and tries to poke through the cracks only she don't find none, and there's everyone warm inside without feelin' no chill except now and again a nice-feelin' shiver runs through their heads when they hear the wind whoop loudest, and that feel good too, man it do," and he stared down the canyon at the yellowed leaves and the stripping trees in the pale sunlight. "Weren't no time to spare neither."

5

WITH WARM AND CONVENIENT living quarters, the partners went back to working the mine and the orderly autumn days passed, crisp with leaves and oval sky bright through branches and deep biting nights that praised the role of the new stove that Dot never allowed to go cold overnight nor during the long working day. Dot's hammer stung with the metal of frost and the snowwhite smoke puffed out of the tunnel stained with the gray-brown of powdered rock, and the ore pile grew. Sometimes Dot would stand and stare with delight at a piece of highgrade with a dreaming grin, singing figures of tonnage and dollars per ton from the custom smelter; Og would listen to the music of the dollars, try to think beyond it and fail.

Dot never quit singing; by day the songs formed formlessly on moving lips in tunes that found tone only by occasional accident but never lost rhythm, and by night, after supper and before bedtime, he would pick up his banjo in a formal recital of the songs that had made themselves during the day as though a physical presence, even unhearing and unappreciating, were all the audience he required:

Somebody else can have
My forty and a mule;
Then he got eighty acres,
And me I ain't no fool.

Big planter own the land,
Then I'm his property,
But if I own my forty,
Then the land own me.

Then another, with the tune altered a little:

Minin' the mine, it suit me fine
I ain't abreakin' no straight line
With ribs all bruised up from the plow;
But every rock I pick up now,
It spend like money at the store.

Or Dot might launch into a story, as though remembering alone a personal incident that had touched him deeply.

"Once I joined up with some hide-hunters, and we went to contractin' meat for the railroad builders. And they's one in this bunch name of Ike: well, he ain't one for gettin' what's comin' to him with work and wits. If he had to do that he'd starve, he would. He ain't no once-in-a-while thief and he ain't no thief that plan good and steal big. He just a natural-born thief. He'd hang up his own hat and steal it from hisself just for the pure thievin' of it. And one mornin' I wake up and my banjo's gone out of the camp and so is Ike. It don't take me long to saddle up for End-of-Track town. Don't take me long to catch up to Ike neither, but I hang back and in town I see him go in and trade that banjo of mine for a great big bottle of whiskey. He ain't the bar-drinkin' kind and he ain't for showin' off what he steal. He like to go off by hisself and look a long time at what he got for his thievin'. So I follow him on out of town again, and when I catch up to him I put my rifle on him and make him get down from his horse. He got a nice little sorrel mare, stole I spose, and a nice new rig on her and a new saddle rifle too and a Remington revolver with a pretty copper powder flask. I spect I'd taken his rope too but I needed it for tyin' him up and this I do. Tie him up so he don't get loose for maybe an hour and then he got to walk — I don't know where to. I take the horse and everything back to town and sell the whole works. Then I go and buy back my banjo and find me some friends, and we share the whiskey and we have us a time, singin', drinkin', banjo-playin' and all."

So the fall days and nights undulated to the uncertain edge of winter paced by the deep dialogue between the two kinds of solitude: Og's far-off secret brooding silence and Dot's overflowing joy evaporating into the vastness.

Deep one night Og exploded out of a sleep that remade the last dynamite shot of the day; but it was not the explosion of powder, only the hammer ringing against the drill like the beat of days on nights and telegraphing muffled shocks through his horn-hard palms. Then one ringing day was lifted out and darkness drew in solidly. The hammer had fallen but didn't ring. It had fallen on Og's skull instead of on the head of the drill and Dot singing and smiling loaded the ore on the wagon and drove to town and sold it, then came back to work his mine on into the riches of his song. It was truly black, with the beating ring gone, black in the cabin and Og could hear Dot snoring loud as blasts. The nigger, then, was snoring and not in town with any ore. Og felt his skull. Yes, the head was whole, the round top of it down over and around his ears to the joining of his neck, except for the face; Og touched his undone face and thought of the black snoring one that had a moment ago been smiling and singing to the hammer that could make Og's head as shapeless as his face.

The long loose time of staring into dark, listening to the pulsing snores, at last brought back sinking sleep. Then the snoring stopped; instead, Dot's big naked feet whispered in the same tempo on the floor toward Og's bunk and the sledge was again in his hand. Og shot back into waking and the snores returned. He stayed awake then until dawn.

There were more such nights looking to the bright common sense of day when Dot would wake up with his grin and beat his first tune with the end of the stove poker in the brittle red coals. Then the day of work would begin: Og plodding and wondering again where his motions might be taking him.

Then smudges from Og's nights began to soil the days. Sometimes when Og held the drill the spaces between clang and jar of hammer fall would stretch until it seemed that Dot held his backswing for moments grinning and deciding between the head of the drill and the head of Og. The sharp sound would tell all, and time would stretch out to the eternity of the next blow. Finally Og demanded to trade tasks with Dot, who handed over the hammer cordially then proceeded to prove that he could make his tunes to the beat of Og's sledge as well as he could to his own.

One night the wind blew strong, blew a river of dry leaves up the canyon noisily colliding with the rush of the retreating stream below, against a pane of glass which Dot and Og had recently nailed tightly into a frame. Stronger gusts played with loose boards and shook sturdy log walls, and in the morning a skin of

snow grew to the ground and rocks and north sides of
the tree trunks and snow still fell, slanting and crossing in a subdued wind.

Dot lifted the stove lid, crushed coals with the shiny
new poker and dropped in a short log from the wood-
box. He waved at the window. "More wood, plenty
more wood out there where we done sweat at the saw-
buck evenings. Ain't it pretty the way she piled out
there side of the house? We use her now and see what
a happy feelin' can get out a plain old stick of wood.
And that wind last night don't find the sneakinest crack
in this cabin I bet. Days like this we live and work for,
when all we got to do the livelong time is set and feed
this stove and watch her snow and blow and be miserable — the more miserable, the better we feels. We
got no boss to make us go down to that black hole
today. It's settin' time and warmin' time and thinkin'
and snoozin' time."

Dot set the coffee pot on the stove, then the iron
skillet with saltside. They ate breakfast, Og silently,
Dot with lip-smacking and grunts. Afterward Dot
without rising skidded his chair back where he could
sit and lean against the wall near the stove, and he
lifted his banjo off the wall, ran his fingers over a bar
and hummed with pressed lips, clear white eyes turned
up to the ceiling. After a while he lifted the stove lid
with one hand, still without rising from the stool or
laying aside his music, and slipped two more logs —
needlessly, Og thought — into the noisy fire. "Yes sir,
days like this a man work the weeks for, and I think
pityin' on those that works the weeks and never gets a
day like this, but they ain't no doin' of mine. My days
is my own doin' and it's always goin' be so."

Og watched Dot, watched silently through the
morning while the snow in the air wore thin and sun
came back, watched the lips close contentedly over a

tune and open capriciously on a song, watched moments of life pass over the black face, happy for all its estrangement, happy with company as without it. Og heard the hammer ring through the other days, ringing whether in his own hands or Dot's and beating as casually as Dot's fingers on the strings. He heard the explosions, the smoke white under a blue sky and the rain of rocks into the night, into the little snatches of sleep and the stark wakings with the hammer repeating in his chest, long dark spaces between; and into this gray recall a bright vivid glimpse of an alone day before the mining time with the silent satisfying hours reaching to the inevitable beat of hoofs, shout of a driver and roll of coach wheels. He thought of the ore. A coach could be bought, a driver hired just to measure solitary days that shut out the hammer clang of banjos and black sweet voices. He thought of the two-man job of drilling for shot, thought of all that Dot had taught him, then saw himself swinging a short sledge and holding the drill in his left hand; slower, but alone, and the ore nestled in its little cavern would wait the slower months as it had waited the centuries, brought out in Og's brief years to buy — something like he might sometime want; Og, still with a face as righteously formless as an unpeopled country but with head intact, unsmashed by a hammer.

The banjo shot out a loud, heavy-handed twang that rattled Og's spine from end to end, shattering thought; and he knew the event was no longer waiting and days away but had begun. He stood up, already alone, and in the deep silence soon to be he had to first make words, "I'm breakin' this partnership off."

The words hadn't sounded at all, for Dot had only shifted his feet on the stove rail and played a shifting run on his banjo; then Og's words came suddenly alive in Dot's asking, Dot never turning his eyes down from the ceiling, "You got money to pay me?" and the question gave life to Og's wrath; he felt his scar-stiff cheek bulge with air as he sounded the single word —

"Pay! Pay you for what?"

Dot thumped the banjo with his palm then tediously began a more thoughtful tune, played his way well into it, picking each note with individual care; his voice was a spoken one but soft as music: "I can't put her down in no black and white because I can't write more'n a figure or two; them three letters make my name and I recollect I got them down on law paper for a share in this claim what's proved up good now, thanks mostly to me, even if I don't say a lie like your work didn't help out a lot; then I puts a dollar in here and there addin' out to maybe two or three hundred. Then I think about a bit of work I done, and my time usta come to some money when I's workin' for a boss. When you come to think about it I don't think you got cash enough on hand to buy me out."

Whenever Og tried to shout the sound came from the torn mouth like a deep roar of wind squeezed between rocks, but somehow he formed words in it. "Can't buy you out, nigger, but I can run you out."

If the heavy fired-out words hit mark they made no showing. Dot's face sobered but didn't anger, any more than it did the time the hammer slipped and struck him full on the kneecap and pain filled the air and should have crossed his eyes but never did; Dot could no more flinch at a word than a hide-hunter at a discharge of his fifty caliber, but he could lift himself finally off his stool as in putting aside pleasure for necessity. This he did, and was on his feet.

The two men stood facing, the lipped black features against the great eye always looking terror. Dot's stare was taking in much more than the eye staring back at him; it was drawing toward the far corner of the cabin where his rifle stood. Then Og began his move.

He turned himself into a crouching one-eyed thing in the space between Dot and the rifle. Then he lunged, but the heel of Dot's right hand lifted his chin and the left hacked sideways and hatchet-like at his throat. Og stumbled backward, his breath shut off, then he recovered and bent forward, drawing and wheezing until he managed to suck some air through his dented windpipe; and Dot's clasped hands dropped like a sledge blow across the top of Og's spine and his body went solid and he looked out through a black blizzard with a hand obeying some life-honoring impulse and closing around the handle of his knife. He saw a black hand flash at his wrist, saw it draw back marked with a wide red gash.

Dot threw himself sideways at the next thrust and the blade nipped the broad end of his nose, then Og's wrist swiveled and the knife retraced its path with a swipe at Dot's abdomen where the buttoned suspenders held the trousers up in a double peak. Og seldom missed but Dot was faster than most. The slash ripped his sweatlined shirt and opened a long shallow gash across his chest.

The knife had completed its downswing and there was an instant to live and decide. Dot decided. He did not use the instant for another lunge at the rifle, to set his more powerful arms, his wide shoulders against Og's knife. He used it to thrust open the door on the blinding glare of noon-melting snow, to spring across the fading white for the dark fringe of trees and the creek where he could have thick cover and perhaps some advantage in attack if Og tried to pursue him.

Og didn't try. He stood in the doorway for a while watching the spot where Dot had disappeared in the branches and shower of wet snow. Then he turned in

45

on the warm gloom of the cabin and shut the door. He stood tasting the new solitude — new and old; the comforting emptiness, silence except for the bubbling fire in the stove eating on the logs Dot had fed it.

All in a moment the cabin was filled with Dot's absence as it had been filled over the months of its creation with his presence. And in that brief moment Og felt his own being in its long-craved solitude escaping as from a faulty container, as warmth might flow from a badly-chinked cabin off into the many directions of cold and over-bright daylight. In something far too close to desperation he fired glances around the room. The dishwater still on the stove; he could throw it out the door and put the washed pots and pans, plates and cups back in their places. The straw broom over in the corner? He could sweep out, get the stove ashes off the floor.

Then he noticed the banjo lying forlornly on its side against the wall. He crossed over to it, lifted it and slowly and deliberately broke it over his knee, broke the neck with his hands and smashed the sounding board with his foot. Then he lifted the lid of the stove and dropped the pieces one by one into the fire.

6

The naked woods wrapped him: in front the glossy tree trunks, the thin lines of snow clinging to bare branches; behind, the dark protecting masses of cedars. Far below, in the broad, whitened hollow, ever-chasing hounds sang in disunity, off key. The clean-damp smells of late night and early winter filled his nostrils; it was starlight cold, and the tough cloth of his work-shirt was thinner than he had ever imagined it to be.

He must have put a good twenty miles behind him since he bolted from the massive shadow of the house into the river trees; a good twenty miles, following the wooded ridges of the Highland Rim. And the hounds he now heard were not the man-tracking hounds. Somebody's pack was loose, chasing a fox most likely. It was good for the moment to listen and think, even with the hunger. Well, hunger was one of the things free meant. And those other leashed hounds nosing the footsteps behind him? He had heard the last of them a night ago, off across a tobacco field on the river flat where the house, the shelter of his boyhood, frowned down from its bluff.

If he had to make the run, why in a snowstorm, with white fields and white woods to show up his black skin? He knew the answer as well now as he had known

it two days ago when he left the house for good: because
things died in winter, and this was when his mother
died too. She wished she could live just a little longer,
she said at the end. She had been a house nigger, had
earned a better life for herself and her little boy — a
life of choice chores around the house, not in the fields.
But she had died despite her wish and Dot was soon
to be sent to the fields. He had not been born to the
fields: he had been born to run away. Now, with him
not yet grown, the time had come and he was a boy
running — but not a boy for long. He figured himself
for close to twelve. He was hungry now. Boys string
out and their guts get long and hard to keep filled up,
she had said. He was very hungry now.

THE HOUNDS YIPPED and crowed — no, the coyotes.
He stood in another winter, in another year and across
another river, looking down from another slope. He
was hungry again.

The night cold slipped through the slit in his shirt
(the slash had been quick and close and the tip of his
nose throbbed where the blade had finally found it);
frosty air surrounded his body, cooling the hot pain.
The twisted bulks of other cedars blended behind with
his black skin, and he watched in front of him, down
the white slope, kept a fix on the cabin and corrals and
the lamplit window. He had come this long way, across
rivers and rivers, to the ocean and back and always
over mountains, to build that house, to stand outside
it in the cold and shiver. "That's the way of things,"
his mother used to say.

The day's snowstorm was over and there would be
no more. The stars were out, solid and white, bright as
they never were in the misty winters of Tennessee:
yonder still, the Dipper with its two stars pointing a

curved finger at The Star. Follow the North Star, after the waiting is over . . . and now the lamp had finally gone out. Wait just a bit longer, eyes still on the cabin and the corrals, the square that stood out below in the field of snow, blackened by hooves.

He moved one cautious step away from the security of the big cedar at his back. The snow squeaked under his foot. The next step he pointed his toe forward until he felt the ground, then let his heel settle. The snow did not squeak. He edged down the slope step by step, occasionally slipping and chilling a bare hand as he braced against a protruding rock, returning the hand to his pocket to warm it against the flesh of his thigh. He must save the warmth; no food to make more, and a long way to go. Right yonder the cabin and corrals and his mule; far off the stars. The waiting, the throbbing wait in the black cold of the cedars was over: the fight and the long, silent day; now the night and the stars.

He approached the corral rails in a crouch, always watching the darkened cabin. That man, the ugly one, warm inside in his bedroll; the other bedroll Dot had occupied last night now empty and cold. He smelled the piñon smoke, saw it, a white wisp standing tall in the still air over the fire Dot had built himself too many days ago to count, for he had never let a fire go out after the first day of autumn chill. But Og had never learned rightly to bank a fire; the stove, the cabin would probably be cold in the morning.

Just in front of him, on the other side of the dim triple line that was the corral, dark forms moved. Og's saddlehorse nickered hunger, head tossing slowly; Dot's mule stood crosslegged, head down, ears back in a doze — a lighter patch against the open end of the shed where the old McClellan saddle would be straddling its log rack, where the mule bridle would be

49

hanging from a nail in the back wall. Dot slipped between the rails. The horse nickered again (would Og remember to throw out hay in the morning?). The mule did not stir as Dot approached him. Dot talked inside his head:

"You knows I'm here, Mule, but you ain't about to let me find out you knows, you cussed critter, standin' there and playin' asleep. Prob'ly don't even grunt none when I cinch up, don't open your mouth for the bit. It's night and sleepin' time, you tell me — ain't goin' wake up till mornin', no matter. You'll doze your way down the trail with me on your back, and that goin' be all right with me too, long as you get a move on. I don't wake you up till mornin'."

His hand was on the warm skin of the mule's neck. It warmed his stiffened hand, warmed him deep. He made his way around the dozing head into the shelter and lifted the bridle off its nail. He lifted the saddle off the log, the blanket under it stiffened with cold and dried sweat. A little way down the trail he would unsaddle, wrap the warmed and limbered blanket around him, and lie down in the snow for a little sleep before daylight. Riding time now, then sleeping time; thinking time would come with the morning.

No sound or stir came from the silent cabin as Dot bridled and saddled as quickly as his chilled hands would allow. Good mule that stood dozing and didn't care a damn: he rocked slowly from side to side as the cinch tightened around him, walked softly behind and halted as Dot let down the corral rails, on out into the snow to turn behind the reins as Dot replaced the rails securely so that the rest of the stock would not stray into the night (the corrals, the shed, the cabin: still home, the place Dot had built; he could not think otherwise just yet). Mule and man walked slowly away from the corral and around the cabin. Dot cared less now for the squeaking of snow underfoot and under-hoof. He could mount and be gone before Og could saddle up and chase after him — if, indeed, Og would even bother to saddle up and chase when he saw that all Dot was doing was taking his mule away. The way Og felt about mules, and especially Dot's mule: he was rid of both of them now — would be in a minute or two, because now Dot mounted and kicked the mule into a slow, jarring trot down the road.

Og, the lone ugly man, he was alone again for sure now. He had won that in a fight that day, and Dot — he had seen to his wounds earlier, seen that they were shallow and slight, though hot and searing as such wounds were, pain enough to let him know he was alive. When there's a fight, somebody's got to win and somebody's got to lose; Dot had come out alive, and alive was the place to start from.

"That's the way of things," he said aloud, and the mule's long ears raised slightly and turned.

The way of things: build a railroad for somebody to ride on, kill and cook meat for somebody to eat, work a mine to get the ore out for somebody . . . build a tight cabin, a warm fire inside. . . . A biting midnight breeze came up and slipped through the rent in his shirt; he hunched his shoulders and drew his arms across his chest and felt the hot diagonal slash.

"The Lord done give and the Lord done took," said Dot and laughed aloud — laughed because something else was supposed to come after that. He couldn't quite recall what, but he knew it would be something to laugh at when he remembered.

The mule plodded around the bend and the cabin was out of sight; a few slow steps later the sideroad turned off to the right and ended a hundred or so feet above at the black hollow in the white hillside. Dot shot a glance aside up to the mine as he passed: a job of work there yesterday; what job of work tomorrow? Wait and see. That was mostly what life was about: Wait and see.

"I got somethin' for a while, then I don't got it no more. Think a man live on this earth a few years don't know about that? You know about that, Mule, and you don't care none. Trouble with bein' a man and not a mule is you gotta care, and when carin's all you can do about it, that's bad. Le'me see now, I got you, Mule, and my pants and a tore shirt. I started out with you and some other things — not countin', say, a coat and hat, which is things that ain't rightly belongin' — you and that there banjo, and I ain't got what I started out with. That banjo: I got me a good mind to turn you around and go knockin' on that there door I made and hung myself, tell that ugly man, 'Look here, I'm takin' along my banjo. You keep the mine and the cabin, but music ain't in your ways, you poor ugly man. You wants the alone livin' so bad you gotta fight to win it. You know how to fight right good, but you don't know how to put to use what you fight for. Any man ain't got music in his ways don't know the use of bein' alone. I'm takin' my banjo.' But then, Mule, what's the use of all that right now? I ain't one to run from no fight, Mule, but I likes to think my years done taught me a little bit of sense — like not gettin' myself into a fight I can't win, him with a knife and all that knife savvy and me with nothin'.' No, I go on my way now, Mule, and wait and see what I goin' do about tomorrow when it get here."

The road steepened and the mule broke again into his wrenching trot. This time Dot pulled him in.

"Now ain't no sense you wearin' yourself down, and me along with you, with all my aches and pains. If'n ever I wanted you to get a move on, you wouldn't. Ain't no bag of grain at the end of this day's run."

The brittle stars seemed to sharpen as the road descended. Another breeze blew, gentle and cold; Dot pinched at the rip in his shirt. Another hour, maybe, and he would have the saddle off, have the blanket off and wrapped around him on the ground before the absorbed warmth of the mule could escape into the night. The night's stop was the next inching step down the new and unknown road. When the mule broke into a trot again, Dot let him go, thinking of the warm blanket around him.

The canyon widened slowly, faithfully under the night sky, as in previous dawnlights of going to town, mules hitched and harness rattling. A sickle moon rose, setting up feeble sparkles in the snow; and abruptly, around a familiar bend, the walled valley floated in moon mist, humped and patched gray with snow-clotted sagebrush and snaked by the black line of leafless trees. This valley, a good enough place to look at now, snowed and moonlit as Dot had never seen it before; a place that put no claim on a man and wouldn't be claimed: a place formed abruptly in the homeless freedom of Dot's life — the contented freedom of moving burdenless when suddenly a few months back the valley had shown itself to him as a place where contentment might remain motionless, a place to come back to and to remember with the knowing that among all the changings of a hundred, a thousand years would be none that could count big in the life of the valley.

Dot unsaddled and tied the mule to a tree. He unfolded the blanket, quickly wrapped himself in the mule's warmth and lay down in the soft snow. Sleeping time now; tomorrow's thinking pushed away to sunup. And he fell quickly into a sound sleep.

He awoke in a blue dawn. In the first instant of waking he knew that a warm morning sun would rise soon and that the snow in the valley would be gone by midday. He sat up and a pain gripped his midsection. Eating time now. But eating time was pushed into another day (perhaps all the days it would take to cross the Big River, follow the Star, and cross the next Big River). He saddled, untied the mule, and mounted.

"You's hungry too, Mule. Yonder's the river (it ain't the Big River though). That's as far as you have to go and ain't even no need for you to cross it. They's dried grass alongside, pokin' up through the snow. I keep talkin' and make you glad yet to be a mule. Grass and a place to drop your head and snooze, 'sall. Don't even know the need for a she. Mule, them's all the wants you got, and that make you a rich man. Me, I ride you into town in a day or so. Folks look up and maybe say, 'That nigger's around again,' and they don't say no more because they got business of their own to tend to. I tend to my business, too, and after while them folks commence to notice my business. They got things to do they don't like to do theirselves — things I can do better than they do and things I don't mind doin' a bit, long's it's only for a little while; they know all this and they willin' enough to pay me to do them things. 'But first,' I say, 'I got to put a little somethin' inside me.' They set me down to eat, then I'm in shape to do the work. Then they's more work, and before you knows it coin commence jinglin' in my pocket. Maybe, with a little somethin' in my belly and coin in my pocket, I gets thinkin' about other things then. That's the way back up from the lowdown times, and I can see somethin' along that way now. Thing is, don't think too far — too far ahead, a man get lookin' that way he see his own tombstone. I thinks a bit at a time, like right now I wants somethin' in my belly; I wants me a warm coat and a hat on my head again. Warm and fed, I maybe wants me some music then. I wants me a banjo. And right there's pretty near all the wants I can calculate up now. You see, Mule, I ain't so poor neither, and I'm mighty near as rich as you. Poor comes from the wantin' of things, not the lackin' of them."

The mule tripped along down the last gentle slope toward the river, hooves breaking thin snow. A rabbit darted from under a clump of sage and gashed a long track off to the tangle of leafless underbrush that marked the river flat. Dot reached under his right thigh and the ends of his fingers slipped into the empty saddle scabbard. The old Henry . . . well, he had been thinking now and then for a long time of trading it off for something newer and better, probably a Winchester. Now it only meant he had nothing to trade off, but the Henry had been hardly worth the trouble of trading. After a new banjo . . . probably a new Winchester; a man needed something to shoot to feel properly that he was his own man; now, the rabbit could as well stand right up out of the brush and laugh at Dot's aching belly.

Hungry, yes, but the pain of his wounds had today become nothing more than a slight stiffness on the surface of the skin, and the vigorous new sun was already on his back, warming him through. Perhaps after the mule got a bellyful of grass Dot could press him into a trot up the tedious rise of road into town. Perhaps man and mule could hold out traveling through the night. Dot took a long pull at the sun-brightened air, as though some of it could possibly seep in and fill the hollow of his stomach, light and nourishing as fresh milk. He patted the mule's neck and tried to remember another hunger of a long time

55

back: it too had ended, across the Big River.

"Grass ahead, Mule, grass ahead! One of us ain't goin' be hungry for long."

The mule plunged down the bank and crossed the narrow flat to the edge of the river. Dot dismounted, dropped the reins, and the mule immediately began to clip seeded tips that protruded through the thinning skin of snow. Birds flashed here and there in the morning sunlight, also feeding on the rich seed that was putting strength into the mule with every crunching mouthful. Everybody, everything hungry on a bright snowy morning beside the fresh gurgle of river, slowly swelling with new trickles from the banks. The new white face of the land that took its color as the sky and seasons gave it; white now, the color of the day and the season, with no voice here to pronounce the word and give it the meaning Dot had learned for it early in his life. He brushed aside the snow and sat down on the bank, patiently letting cold dampness come through the seat of his pants as he looked around him. It was country to smile at, a day to grin with — a day for music, if he had his banjo. Perhaps for the moment he could understand something of that craving of the man Og. Stripping away the discomforts of the moment and the situation — letting them evaporate into the clear white silence — it was a little bit good to be alone again.

The grazing mule worked his way down the bank, and when he was about to disappear around the bend, Dot got up and followed. A new spot, another half hour or so of sitting with empty mind, then on down the river as the mule put mouthful after mouthful of the seeded grass into his stomach.

"Come, Mule, it's time we got on our way to town."

Dot picked up the reins and mounted. The mule hastily nipped off his parting mouthful of grass tips

56

and, chewing around the working bit, climbed the
bank and plodded on up the road. An old tune of his
came to Dot's mind, and he fitted some new words to
it, running them through his head once, then singing
aloud.

> Across the River is where I be,
> Across the River from Tennessee;
> It's a long, long road I ride, Mule,
> With a big, black hollow inside;
> It's a long, long road I've traveled down,
> And a long, long way into town.

He sang the words one more time, then knotted
his reins together and draped them over the pommel.
Right hand strumming the air and fingers of the left
nimbly working imaginary strings, he sang the song
a third time.

"Time I gets into town, I'll have me a new song
made, banjo or no . . . new words, is all; can't make
no kind of tune without that there banjo."

Dot passed the miles, plucking slowly, fingering
frantic runs, or fanning wildly, singing low and sweet,
or at the top of his large voice. In between, he listened
in reverent respect to the long silences of the country
around him in its daylight winter sleep. The sun passed
the noon of its northern arc and started to fall.

"Now why is I still hungry, Mule, when I done had
me a good breakfast this mornin' and just stopped
and had me a bite at noon?" He paused thoughtfully,
then laughed. "What I really wanted to ask you is,
if'n I can imagine me up a good banjo that play right
good, why can't I imagine me a good breakfast and
a bite of noontime in my belly? Guess I'll be hungry
from now on, as long as I lives, and I got to learn to
see it that way. One thing, it don't hurt like it did

this mornin'. It hurt a little less every day; I knowed that once and now I knows it again."

Daylight passed into a brief winter dusk. The country had risen slowly, and the first few pines appeared in the shelter of low hills. The snow, probably gone by this time in the lower country, thickened stubbornly. Streams of chill air flowed around in silent gasps.

"Gotta sing more, Mule; gotta sing you plumb into town."

The dusk passed quickly into a clear, cold night packed with stars. The cold was stiffening his bare hands around the reins, numbing the fronts of his legs, and paining his feet. No longer were his hands and arms limber enough to play the banjo. He dismounted in the shelter of a clump of stubby pines, unsaddled, and accepted gratefully the warmth of the unfolded blanket.

"It's sleepin' time, Mule — always sleepin' time and ridin' time and never eatin' time; them times done got mixed up someways."

A colder dawn came in the more advanced winter of this higher country, and Dot shook himself out of the blanket in the snow and quickly saddled. Something would happen to him before the solid night formed again. He quickened inside: the old, old feeling was upon him — the going, the wait-and-see, the unexpected match for his wits waiting at the end of another road. Town was only a few hours' ride now, and the mule, slowed now by fatigue and hunger, swung into his plodding walk while Dot sang his way along the slowly mounting road. He pressed on through midday, measuring with his eye as the pines in the hollows grew and thickened, clotted more and more heavily with snow.

And as time and miles lengthened, his mind darted

backward for fleeting glimpses of the mine, of the cabin and Og, and day before yesterday.

"Most of all, Mule, I wants to live, and I's particular about what I lives with. Now like, I couldn't live with the shootin' of a man sneakin' from off'n the side of a hill, say."

He was riding deeper into the dusk, between coldly lit and silent buildings with dim life in their orange windows, past hotel and faint winter life of saloon, on down to the end of the street and through the gate of the livery stable corral. He dismounted and walked to the little shed at the end of the row of dark, stirring stalls. The door opened to his knock. A man stood in the frame in his dirty, wrinkled socks and looked Dot up and down from his position some five inches below Dot's eyebrows. Then he stepped aside and motioned Dot in. The room was small, warm, and filled with the smells of food, coffee, and stale bed-clothing that easily overpowered the cold odors of manure, urine, hay, and horseflesh from outside. With a small, frantic jerk the man closed the door against the cold.

"I wants to put up my mule and hay and grain him," said Dot. "I done had me a long ride, Winnie."

Winnie stood fidgeting in front of Dot, looking him over again, from hatless head to mud-caked shoes. The pinched little face was full of questions that Dot knew the diffident Winnie would not ask. The questions would stay in the face, which was itself a small question.

"Long ride," Winnie's crackling voice repeated after Dot. His eye came to rest on Dot's ripped shirt with scabbed flesh showing through. "And it's a cold night, ain't it?" One corner of his mouth jerked in a half smile and the eye above it winked with the spasm. He pointed to the table. "Coffee?" he invited. "Maybe a plate of pork and beans. I'm just finishing up supper."

Dot felt his stomach lurch with each word Winnie spoke, and the pain again crossed his middle. He shrugged and grinned.

"Coffee, maybe — to warm up a bit. Might be could eat a bite with you just to be company." He stretched indifferently and sat down on the nail keg at the plank table that had never been meant to accommodate more than one diner. "How long you been shut up here? Looks like you'd a found somebody to mind the stable, with all them big times up town."

"Up town?" A slow smile turned up both sides of Winnie's mouth.

"Saloon's plum lively . . . girls in there and cacklin' like a henhouse at sunrise."

"Girls? . . . Well, *ain't* nobody but me to mind the stable. I got a business to run, y'know. Why else'd I be here, nights and nights and nights all by myself; don't you think that can drive a man crazy?"

Dot fell upon his plate of beans, restraining his movements with effort while his slowly filling stomach called frantically for more. Winnie slumped dejectedly over the half-filled tin cup of coffee. Dot raised his left hand slowly to scratch his ear, then let the hand fall to the table with a thud. Winnie gave a sudden, toadlike leap on his nail keg.

Dot's eyes squeezed in laughter. "Man, you's spooky as a catch colt. A drink or two'd take them jumps out of you."

Winnie always jumped at sudden sounds when he had no whiskey in him. The drinks, Dot knew, were the only cure — for the jumps and the twitch in his face. Dot waited.

"But I tell you," Winnie whined, "there's nobody to mind the stable if I go out for a drink."

Dot continued to eat slowly, letting the small anguish work a bit longer on Winnie. Finally he said,

"Seems I recollect times when havin' nobody to mind the stable didn't stop you . . . only you didn't just go upstreet for no drink; you gone upstreet for maybe three, four days, and old Merryweather . . . Well, maybe you a little bit owner of this stable, but old Merryweather, he a whole-lot owner, like he is with just about everythin' else in town. And he come around and find you gone and man, do he get mad! He tell you if'n you don't shape up you ain't even goin' be a little bit owner no more."

The name of Merryweather the Banker was terror to many. Winnie's body sagged with the small, defeated face turned down to the table.

"I didn't say I'd go off on one of them things again," he muttered. "I'm all through with that. I was just figurin' maybe you'd watch after things a while if I went up street and come right back."

"But supposin', just supposin' you's to stay away till, say, midnight. It'd be nice to know they was somebody around that'd look after things good."

Winnie straightened up hopefully. "I'd be back in an hour." The smile and wink gave the lie to the firm promise in the voice.

Dot did not answer. He finished his plate of beans, wiped his mouth on the back of his wrist, and glanced at the pot of coffee on the stove. Then he leaned back and stared at the ceiling.

Winnie jumped up obligingly and took the pot off the stove.

"Want some more beans?"

"I ain't all that hungry, but might be I'd eat a bit more if'n you's to spoon it out."

Winnie poured Dot's coffee and hopped to the bean pot with Dot's empty plate.

"I'd only be gone maybe two hours." Winnie managed somehow to fight back the wink.

Dot sipped at Winnie's sour coffee. He said slowly, "I don't reckon I'd much care if'n you's to be gone the night. I'd do what chores needs doin' and crawl into that there bedroll, I's that tired out."

Instantly Winnie was a flurry of jerky movements. He reached his sag-brim wool hat from the back of the door and fitted it to his head like a sunbonnet. He squirmed into his oversized coat and his hands disappeared in the hanging cuffs, then he sat down on the nail keg to pull on his boots with upturned toes.

"And I don't reckon . . . " Winnie halted abruptly at Dot's voice, a boot poised in midair. ". . . that a dollar, say, wouldn't be too much wages to look after the stable, feed and groom in the mornin' and all. A dollar ain't much pay, but the feed and stall for my mule'd make out the rest."

With visible relief, Winnie finished pulling on his other boot. He was on his feet, his hand on the doorlatch. "I might stay a couple, two three hours. I'll pay you for the time."

"Worth it, I'd say," said Dot, "keepin' old Merryweather off'n your back. . . . Now I ain't sayin' you'd do it, mind, but if'n you's to stay away all day tomorrow, even all night next night and all day next day, you'd know the stable was bein' looked after good, and if'n old Merryweather or somebody come in I'd say you was upstreet a bit and things around here was fine. You know a dollar a day ain't much in wages, dear as things is gettin' in this town, but I ain't got much to take up my time these winter days."

Winnie shut the door on Dot's last word and was gone, his short steps fading into the night outside. Dot grinned, got up and spooned another plate of beans, fishing out some large chunks of sidemeat. Sleepy warmth rose like a vapor out of his stomach and filled his head. When he had finished eating he went outside, led his tired mule to an empty stall, unsaddled and unbridled, dipped grain into the feedbox and pitched a few generous forkfuls of hay into the manger, and covered the stall floor with dry bedding straw. When he stepped back into the small room he glanced at Winnie's narrow bunk. He sat down on it and unlaced his shoes. Stripped to his underwear, he stood up, lifted the lamp off its ceiling hook and blew it out. It would take Winnie a good full night just to find something to do in the winter-dulled town, two more nights to do it in, and at least a day to recover and find his way back to the stable. Dot fell asleep on the thought.

In the morning, filled with a good oatmeal breakfast, Dot saw to his mule and the few horses in the stalls. He spent some time grooming until the sun rose high in the clear sky — a comfortable enough day for a man without a coat to take a short walk up the street and look briefly into the days beyond the day that Winnie would return and pay him, say, the three dollars he would have earned. There would be other jobs — more as the winter deepened and folks got lazy around the warm stoves. He would pick up coin here and there, and the winter would be gone into spring by and by. In his memory he saw the valley again. Might be there were other mines. . . .

He started off up the deserted street, past the saloon, and stopped at the window of the loan shop. There, among the revolvers and rings, rifles and lodge pins, packsaddles and mine tools, in the very center of the haphazard display of bad luck, stood a banjo. It was not nearly as good a one as . . . but it would make music, and most likely nobody would be looking to buy it before the time Dot could put enough coin in his pocket to bargain with.

"The Lord done give and the Lord done took."

And at that moment he remembered the rest of it.

" 'Praised be the Lord.' . . . A banjo right yonder."

It had come straight out of the squirmy Sunday mornings of his boyhood, looking down from the slave gallery into the great hollow filled with heads hatted and hatless, with masters and missuses, storekeepers and lawyers from the town, the poor-but-honest among the white folks; looking down on the bald head in the pulpit — the head with a voice talking about work and obedience. Talking to the masters and missuses with his face, but talking upward into the galleries with his voice.

Dot had kept on squirming. He had taken his mother's cuffs on the ear silently, and squirmed some more. He had wriggled and squirmed through boyhood days, until there were no cuffs on the ear, nobody to care whether he squirmed or ran. He could have run with the others, who planned carefully in the night and met and talked under the gums and sycamores without lamplight. But he had run alone. That was the way of things — his way of things.

"The Lord done give and the Lord done took. . . . Poor ugly man. Poor, poor ugly man."

The battered banjo with its tarnished metal and scuffed soundingboard became a more and more pleasing sight as his eyes stayed on it. A tune began to make itself in his head — a new tune, the first new one in . . . he tapped his foot. The rhythm came first and the tune formed around it, fleshing out the rattling bones of the rhythm. It wouldn't be long now, and he hummed the tune. Then the words, and he sang softly:

> All things got their seasons,
> They does, they does;
> And seasons all comes back again,
> Just like they was.

7

Og LIVED ALONE IN THE CABIN through the winter. Snow fell a few more times, and once when the sun was lowest in the southern sky a snowfall remained three full days on the ground, blunting the sharp rocks and hiding brittle tips of taller grasses until its surface was sown with the seeking of birds and gashed long and straight with the flight of rabbits and the preying of foxes and coyotes. But even after the whitest of days, after the brief snows quit falling, the sky was always uncovered blue, and in the latter days when clouds did enter they crossed the sky rapidly, occasionally pausing to dust the earth and soon disappearing over the dipping eastern skyline, leaving the sky to its clear, pale winter.

Those days just after Dot left, the snow gone with him for the time being, were bright and biting-dry over a moistened earth, and Og used none of them for work in the mine. He sat inside the cabin, going out only for wood and water and stock-feeding, stoking the stove frugally and receiving the scant warmth it returned. He was soon back to eating two meals a day, often uncooked, thinking of Dot's eulogies on good cooking which he was probably still giving, hunched off alone someplace over a fire and talking on as though he had never left company; and with food put hastily into himself, the chore of it out of the way, Og would put Dot quickly out of his mind.

In later days Og managed to make his way to the mine, having aroused some kind of appetite for work which vanished as soon as he rediscovered the dark hole hidden in the curve of rock. He squandered half a day hefting tools and laying them down, scratching idly at the lips of the opening with a sterile pickax. Then he had a sudden craving to hear, as before, a dynamite blast thump into the arrogant rock. He tried swinging the sledge against a drill and found it clumsy. He sawed short the handle of the sledge, wrapped it with thong, took up the drill, and by evening he had placed a wasteful charge and set it off. The sound, the sight, the feel of destroying strength roused him briefly, but by nightfall he was left only with the drab thoughts of shoveling and grading, the dusty dumping onto the growing pile of gravel clinging to the creek bank below the tunnel and graying and choking the clear moving water. The following days he managed to draw some work from himself by driving and thinking toward the firing of each shot which would bring the blood pounding pleasantly into his skin, draw all living and feeling into one instant: lighting the fuse, anticipating behind the shielding rock down the slope beside the gravel dump for the magnificent crash and grand display of gushing smoke and shaken earth, the one great indulgence he had learned from Dot to enjoy but which he could only fully enjoy alone.

But he must earn each of these moments with the humdrum drudgery between shots, the common deadening routine which the moment itself created, so that eventually Og's mining came to consist merely of setting off one blast after another and cleaning up after each one to drill for another.

One morning when he had harnessed the two great brooding mules and was about to drive them to the mine to drag out some of the accumulated drift, one of the animals casually kicked him in the back of the knee as he was picking up the trace chains. His stomach went sick with pain and his mind went cold and vacant as the winter sky. He limped around to the huge haughty heads and stuck each mule in the large vein of the neck with his knife then backed away while first the jack then the mare collapsed, thrashed together in harness, and lay still. He then unbuckled and removed the harnesses, took them to the spring and rubbed off the copious drenching of drying blood. Then, using the one animal left in the corral, his saddle horse, he dragged each carcass singly upstream away from his cabin, where wolves would be sure to find the fresh meat and coyotes and buzzards would clean the bones for the polishing winds.

He started again for the mine, but when he had moved downstream as far as the cabin he found himself with no will to go on to work just yet. He turned the horse into the corral and took himself inside the cabin to drain the last of the coffee out of the grounds in the pot and sip with no enthusiasm at the luke-warm, sour brew. He slipped a log into the stove. He was down on the stool again, and days went by before he again got himself down to the mine with the horse to discover, after dragging hours, that the haul from all the rousing days of blasting was a small fraction of what he and Dot together used to take out in a single day's work. Then one look up at the sky told Og in an instant that winter was nearly spent, that the sun was three quarters on its way back from the south. Spent — in countless hours before the half-cold stove sipping unwanted coffee, eating little-wanted food, mind vacant and drifting unproductively with the slow seeping of time.

The next day Og loaded on the wagon all the ore he estimated the light-boned, mine-weary saddle horse could haul and took a quick inventory of the leavings of the last load of supplies from town. Then he discovered that the extravagance of his passion in slaughtering the mules was going to demand a tedious price, and grumbling soundlessly he set to the task of removing the doubletree from the wagon hitch and re-rigging the hitchings for a single animal; yes, and the one mule harness he had been using on the saddle horse to drag out the drift was, despite his many cuttings, punchings, resplicings of leather, still far too large for the animal. It had already worn galls in the flesh, and the horse would probably be a mass of them before half the journey to town was completed, and Og would have to stop often and cut patches to slip under the harness to ease the pain and soreness if the miserable animal were to be able to complete the trip. His hands remained busy, demonstrating in pantomime the petty movements of his thoughts but tracing a digressive course. The following day he agreeably drove toward the wagon road, strangely eager to put mine, cabin, the far canyon, the desolate valley behind for a few days.

He unloaded the ore at the railroad and drove the empty wagon back down the main street, his eye aligning the stores he would need to visit that day, planning each stop, each necessary purchase like a marketing farm wife. The last shreds of the old, old dread thinned — the dread of many faces, many voices, scuffing feet. The first truly powerful decision seized him: his first stop would be the saloon.

Several pairs of eyes stared from along the porched

front of the wooden hotel; half a dozen wagons stood idle in the early spring dust along the fringes of the street. Og had no craving for a drink, but the saloon doors drew him, their slow double swing beckoning in the light breeze. He tied his harnessed horse to the rail, swung up to the boards of the walk, and pushed into the big, dark, sour room for the ration of two drinks he had set for himself.

Time slowed, and the room expanded around him when he stepped through the doors, but the first drink he sipped began to draw the walls a trifle closer. When he had finished the drink he stood comfortably alone in an intimate room, losing himself in the genial maze of mars and scrapes, dark scratches and white rings on the bad varnish of the bar. The mine, the canyon, the valley, the road — now the town itself was shut out. He made no effort to discover whether this new kind of seclusion were truly satisfying; it was most certainly not unpleasant: it resembled somewhat the content-ment he had known throughout the days before he had left the employ of the Stage Line. So complete was the shutting in that it was long minutes, like hours or days, before he began to be aware of the merged murmur off to his left — the voices of fellow drinkers.

The voices seemed at first to come through a wall so surely opaque that Og did not consider looking to-ward them; when he did so by accident, casual as the lifting of his glass, he saw that a group of men stood just off his right elbow. The men seemed to be all talk-ing at once, none listening to what another was saying, and occasionally a grouped laugh erupted, like the single motion of a startled herd. The wall that formed Og's private drinking chamber was slowly dissolving.

Then the saloon went abruptly silent as the doors to the street parted just enough to let in a slender, slouching figure. The eyes of the bar drinkers fixed on him and followed as he strode in hunching steps to one of the card tables on the side of the room opposite the bar. The man's thinness was emphasized by the large broadcloth coat that sagged off the ends of his shoulders and hung unevenly halfway to his knees. The face was narrow and elliptical, sharply pointed at the lower end and bisected by a mustache so wide it very nearly matched the length of the face, which disappeared at its upper end into a slouch-brimmed, crush-crown hat.

Grins flicked on and off like struck matches among the group as the man sat down at the table, removed a small leatherbound book from his coat pocket, and opened it on the table. The single stare of the several pairs of eyes broke apart as the men at the bar exchanged brief looks and grins. Then one of them, distinguished largely by the fact that he was some three inches taller than the rest and had a torso shaped like a giant beanpod, stepped away from the others like a single member of a troupe about to give a solo performance. He walked about halfway to the table where the newcomer sat.

"Why, hullo there, Professor."

The man at the table, trying with little success to give no evidence that he heard the shouted greeting or was aware of the greeter's presence, did not look up from his book. Og, hearing the greeting, began to put together from unremembered places bits of information that constituted his own knowledge of the Professor. Whatever his name may have been in another place or places, the Professor needed no other here. Having lived in the town for more than a year he could be considered a long-time resident; he occupied a small room behind the drygoods store and millinery shop, had no employment or known interest in any, and often visited the saloon, always with a book. Frequently, and on occasions such as the one that seemed about to be, he played the role of entertainer — a role not of his own making, but one he performed as directed by those entertained. Being forced to play the role repeatedly did not deter him from returning to the saloon again and again, and the mystery of his remaining in the town and frequenting the saloon under such conditions had added a dimension to the interest his public showed him. It had become something of a challenge, a challenge that stood through repeated takers, to discover what the Professor was indeed doing here — where he came from and where, if anyplace, he was going. Og found himself caught up in the air of expectation that hung heavy in the room.

"I said hullo, Professor. . . . How's your hammer hangin'?"

Beanpod had taken two more steps forward with his second greeting. At last the Professor found it impossible to keep up his pretense of not hearing. He looked up from his book and raised his eyebrows.

"I beg your pardon."

"Ain't nothin' to pardon, Professor. I just said hullo and how's your hammer hangin' — or ain't you got one?"

The Professor smiled wearily. "I don't understand the nature of your question; I therefore can't give you a proper answer."

"Don't matter none, Professor. If'n you ain't got one, you can't much tell me about how it's hangin'." Beanpod moved over to the table and peered at the book. "What's them funny letters?"

"*Them* is a pronoun," said the Professor, again bending to his book and shaking his head slowly.

Beanpod straightened up to a posture of indignation.

"Now I don't mind you don't answer a question you can't. But when I ask you one you can, I want a

71

right sort of answer to it. But what do you do? You answer me in them fancy words so's I can't understand. Now I want you to tell me just like folks what is them funny letters."

The group maintained its waiting silence, faces strained in grins, ready to burst into unanimous laughter when their time came. The Professor leaned back in his chair, placed his hands flat on the table, and looked up at the big man.

"If I thought you were truly interested, I should be more than pleased to tell you — indeed, translate aloud some of this magnificent work for you. But your present manner indicates no such interest. In time, the inevitable change will come to you and all others in this place. Civilization will surely follow closely behind me, and its blessings will become known. Then I shall read aloud to you from this and other works in my library."

Displaying still more of his natural theatrical skill, Beanpod allowed another measure of indignation to enter his voice and his face: "You sayin' I ain't civilized?"

A few undisciplined chuckles escaped the group.

"Not so," said the Professor patiently. "Civilization is not a quality or property that may be attributed to any one man. It is a condition — a blessing, as I have named it, of which we all partake when it is available to us; unhappily, it is a condition that does not yet exist in this place and thus, through no fault of your own, you do not partake of it."

Beanpod took a sideways step and stood directly over the Professor's chair.

"But you did say I ain't fitt'n to hear readin' from your goddamn book. You did say such, didn't you?"

The Professor shook his head. "I most certainly did not intend to imply such a thing. You are not inherent-

72

ly unfit; it is the benighted condition of which you are a prey that renders you unfit. You are merely a blameless victim."

Beanpod slowly scratched his jaw, studying the Professor's upturned face, then he lowered his hand to his belt. With both hands, he eased backward the edges of his coat until he revealed the scratched and gouged wooden handles of two revolvers hanging in scabbards.

"I guess it's my friends you're talkin' about, then. They ain't fit folks, you say."

The Professor stared a moment at the revolvers then, eyes a little wider than before, looked back up into the big square face.

"No, no. Not at all," he protested rapidly. "They too are victims. But there is hope, friend. A new day is soon to come to this land." The Professor's voice had risen a tone higher than its normal high pitch, the pattering words touched lightly by impatience and apprehension.

"Then we ain't none of us fit for nothin'. But we got hope. You or Jesus, one, will save us."

The first truly unified laugh broke from the group at the bar, with slapping of thighs and a few delighted yips.

"I have no particular belief in Jesus, except as a great teacher. It is mankind that must save itself, and not rely on some contrived supernatural being. Therein lies my faith. We must place our faith in what men can do together, each as a small part of the Great Soul."

Beanpod turned to address his audience. "He says we ain't fit, and he says Jesus ain't fit neither. I bet he wouldn't read that goddamn book of his to Jesus hisself."

The laughter was cut short when Beanpod turned again to resume his performance.

"Now I tell you what, Professor. I don't take no insults like that and especially when you insult my friends and Jesus too. Now you and me is gonna fight it out right here and now, just to see who's fit."

The Professor's head-shaking grew more and more rapid as Beanpod talked, and it continued to shake, mustache flapping, into the long silence that followed. The mass at the bar was again fixed in cohesive, quiet waiting.

"I . . . I . . . " The Professor fought for his voice, which had risen so high it had nearly escaped him. "I am a man of peace. Violence has no part in human civilization, and I refuse to participate in the violence that characterizes the uncivilized state that surrounds me."

"This ain't no state yet, it's a territory. You may be an educated man, but there's a thing or two you don't know."

The Professor's eyes kept moving rapidly from Beanpod's face to the exposed brace of revolvers; he apparently had no wish this time to correct the man's error. He seemed to see little significance in the obvious difficulty Beanpod was having stifling a grin.

"I wouldn't expect the likes of you to have no gun." Beanpod was easing his lefthand revolver out of its scabbard. "So I'm gonna be bighearted and give you one of mine. Now, it's a gift. It's all your'n, and you can use it if'n you want. That's up to you. But it's only the right thing to tell you that I'm gonna use the one I'm keepin' for myself."

Beanpod laid the revolver down beside the open book. The Professor stared at it as he might have at a snake. The two objects, nearly touching: the russet leather binding and giltedged pages of the book and the worn Navy Colt, the ribs of its octagon barrel streaked with faint rust stains; only briefly did he glance up at the row of grins, the merged delight of expectation along the bar, only briefly at the artfully grim face of Beanpod, whose right hand was now fumbling, first in the pouch at his belt, then with the cylinder of the revolver still in the scabbard at his right side. After allowing a tense silence, Beanpod said,

"Well, it looks like you ain't gonna use that there gun, Professor. Man gives you a gift and you ain't the good manners to use it. But I made a promise and I gotta keep my promises. That's only good manners, y'see. I promised to use the gun I kept, and now I gotta do it. Too bad . . ."

He eased the other revolver out of its scabbard, leveled it, slipped the hammer back, and placed the muzzle against the Professor's temple, the barrel lifting slightly and supporting the absurd slouch brim of the hat.

"Now it ain't like the sort of man I am not to give you a decent bit more of time, like maybe countin' to ten. . . . One . . . two . . . "

The monotone counting paced the slow silence of the room. The Professor sat in the submissive hunch of a dog about to be kicked, staring forward as though already stunned by the blow.

" . . . ten." Beanpod squeezed. The hammer fell and the small, sharp sound startled the room as the cap he had just slipped onto the nipple exploded into an empty chamber.

The Professor's head jerked at the sound, then nodded forward. The death silence held a few seconds. Then Beadpod gave the cue. He hunched over, gun-hand hanging, and bobbed up and down with a whispered, wheezing laugh. Just off Og's right elbow the great roar sounded in his ear like a dynamite blast out of the mouth of the mine as the spark crawling up the fuse finally detonated the mass of laughter.

The Professor shook his head sharply, took a linen handkerchief from his pocket, unfolded it, and mopped at his forehead.

Beanpod recovered slowly from his seizure: "I knowed that chamber was empty."

"You *knew* it was empty," gasped the Professor, folding his handkerchief and replacing it in his pocket.

"That's what I said." Beanpod let another small fit of laughter pass. "I knowed all the time it was empty because I fired it out at a rabbit this morning. Hit him square, too. But you wasn't watchin' good, Professor, or you'd a seed me slip that cap on the empty. You're all right, Professor, and I'm gonna buy you a drink right now." He motioned to the bar.

The bartender brought a bottle and two glasses to the table. The Professor seized the bottle, poured three fingers, and gulped it before Beanpod could sit down and pour a drink. The group at the bar drifted slowly over, carrying glasses, and surrounded the table, chuckles of satisfaction bursting out here and there among them. Beanpod's successful performance had clearly ended. Og was alone at the bar.

"Perhaps now," said the Professor, catching his breath as though he had joined in the laughter, "I shall read you a little from this book." He cleared his throat. "Translating from the German, it's . . . "

"Maybe tomorrow, Professor. Can't use your mouth for readin' and drinkin' at the same time, y'know."

Og's solitary chamber at the bar had begun again to close around him. He watched as the Professor, Beanpod, and the rest poured drinks and tipped up their glasses. He saw the Professor pour two more in succession and gulp them down; now, it seemed, the Professor had truly joined them — even in the laughter. Og watched until his solitude finally shut him away again.

He quit the saloon to make his rounds for supplies, haggle for a team of horses, load, harness, and leave the town. Dark overtook him in a few miles, and he made camp and drove on to the canyon the next day.

He had a small sack of money to be added to his tin box and a good load of supplies, including plenty of dynamite. As he drove up the road to his mine and cabin, eagerness to return to his new pleasure grew large. The day was past middle when he pulled up before the cabin, and he took only the scantest of minutes to unload and unharness; then he hurried down to the waiting hole and attacked with drill and sledge. He measured a shallow hole, impatient to place the shot and set off the blast; he loaded the hole, which was not deep enough to achieve anything in terms of getting out ore, lit the fuse and scrambled for cover. The explosion came faithfully; so did Og's echoing roar of laughter, his gleeful shouts, his absurd babbling that continued to outdo the dying rumbles of spent powder and unceasing chatter of the stream.

When it was over, he flew into a silent rage. He suddenly knew that this laughter, shouting and babbling of his had become as predictable and involuntary a part of the dynamite blasts as the echoes and reverberations. The image of Dot was before him — Dot, bent double with squinted eyes and open mouth, yipping and cackling his greeting to the first shot ever fired in the mine. He quit his work then and there to return to his cabin for a tasteless meal, a disturbed night's sleep.

The next morning, with no breakfast, he went back to the mine to try again. He prepared a shot hole even more hastily, packed it and strung out the fuse. He stood long with the match in his hand. He would not make the sounds this time. He took a deep breath, clamped his crooked jaws together, and lit the fuse.

But the crawling spark took its own usual time to travel the length of the fuse. Time weakened Og's guard. The explosion came, strong and full and deep down the throat of the tunnel, voicing itself outward until the canyon walls and farther hills shook with it. Og heard his own voice reply out of the slitted, re-made mouth. He stopped abruptly and stood shaken, and the shaking continued into a rage.

In another week Og was back in town, filled with thoughts he found hard to identify with the self he knew. Perhaps he would buy a small flock of chickens and have fresh eggs in the morning when the stove was warm in the false frost of spring; maybe he would get a few head of beef and drive them back onto the flat above the mine where the wild timothy headed out waist high in the summer, and their bawling would sound down the canyon on moonlit nights — sounds and smells of something more than a mine camp for a lone man out here off this valley that had thus far re-jected all men but himself; something to hear and feel on sleepless nights. Maybe . . . but at the moment he was in the saloon with a half-wanted drink in his hand.

A lively bit of business was there that noontime. Small groups of smaller purpose were scattered along the bar and about the room. Talk was quiet and the occasional laughter was diluted and disunited.

Og took a narrow room at the hotel that night and kept himself to it until well into the next day, peer-ing often out the tiny rear window down into the stable where he had left his team. Turning from the window, he stared at the rocking chair, the commode chest with white ironstone pitcher and basin and the bright, knobbed brass bed and thought of his cabin. He might buy a few sticks of furniture to take back . . .

A little after noon he walked out onto the wide, bright street.

When he pushed open the doors of the saloon, it was as though he had arrived just in time for the show. The same audience was lined up along the bar with waiting faces — the same faces, as nearly as Og could distinguish them, that had burst apart in laughter that other time. There, too, were the principals: Beanpod had already walked his several steps away from his companions and drawn the line between performer and audience; at his table, open volume spread in front of him, head bent in simulated concentration, sat the Professor.

"Now it ain't gonna be like before," Beanpod was saying; "I'm gonna have me a look at that there book today, Professor, and we'll see am I fit to read them letters."

The Professor looked up. "Oh, but this is not the book to which you have reference. I shall gladly read to you from this book."

Beanpod took another step forward. "That won't be necessary, Professor, because I'm gonna read it myself. Now they taught me good to read and write in the Army."

The Professor smiled. "It's not your ability to read that I doubt; it's your ability to give proper expression to these words. Now I'll read . . ."

The Professor bent his head and cleared his throat. But with a sudden lunge and sweeping grasp Beanpod had the book in his hands. He backed off, holding the open book close to his face and studying it.

"Now this is right nice . . . Poetry . . . "

"If you will please give the book back to me, I'll . . . "

"Oh, I can't do that. I'm plumb took with it now."

Beanpod peered over the top of the book at his audience, who were now preparing faces for the opening laugh. "And it ain't for the likes of you, neither, you uncivilized coyotes. Only for the Professor and me."

The Professor continued his plea. "If you will only give the book back to me, I can enhance the appreciation you have already begun to feel. I can ably convey to you the grace of Milton."

"Not likely, Professor, not likely." Beanpod brought the book close to his face and furrowed his forehead. "Grace . . . she's right in there, sure enough." He lifted his other hand above his head, letting it fall from a loose wrist with fingers pointing at the crown of his hat, and began to prance his big body lightly back and forth across the room to some slow, contrived rhythm in his head, lifting his huge thighs high, like a dray-horse attempting to imitate blooded saddle stock.

"Dang if it ain't right purty . . . Now listen here, I'm readin' . . . it says right here . . . it says," Beanpod softened his voice, affecting a slight lisp; then he began,

"Sweet was the sound, when oft, at evening's
      close,
   Up yonder hill the village mur . . . mur . . ."

The Professor jumped to his feet. "But . . . you've turned pages, lost my place. . . . That is *not* Milton. That's Goldsmith."

"Don't matter none, Professor," said Beanpod, a little annoyed. "Grace Milton, Grace Goldsmith . . . don't matter none. Now listen to my readin' and mind your manners." He resumed,

"There, as I passed with careless steps and slow,
   The ming . . . mingl . . ."

"Mingled," prompted the Professor, sitting down again.

" . . . notes came softened from below;
The swain res . . . resp . . ."

"Reseponsive." The professor finished the line,
" '. . . as the milkmaid sung.' I only wish that you would
give me back the book so that . . . "

"Can't be did, Professor," said Beanpod, the hoarse-
ness of his conversational voice contrasting with the softened tones of his reading voice. He went on, seeming
at last to have achieved a stride, as though he had suddenly reacquired the skill of reading:

"The sober herd that lowed to meet their
    young;
The noisy geese that gabbled o'er the pool,
The playful children just let loose from school;
The watch-dog's voice that bayed the whisp . . .
    whispering wind,
And the loud laugh that spoke the vacant
    mind."

Finished, Beanpod took a large breath and looked
again over the top of the book at the uncertain faces
of his listeners.

"Now listen here. I'm gonna tell you fellers what
that there's sayin'. That's sayin' right now, if'n you go
to laughin' *too* loud, then you ain't got nothin' in your
head."

He pranced the width of the room several more
times, lips moving silently as he continued to study the
book with a frown; he finally came to rest at the bar,
leaning on an elbow with the book still close to his
face as though he had genuinely gained some affection
for it as an object. The Professor watched apprehen-
sively, it being apparent that a new and unexpected
phase of the performance was about to begin. The line
at the bar allowed itself some guarded, disunited

laughter, still restrained by the certainty that the biggest moment of all was about to come.

Then Beanpod let the book fall from his hand; it dropped with a plosh into the flaring bronze mouth below. Beanpod followed its fall with his eyes and shook his head.

"Dang. Now lookut there. That purty book and all them purty words fallen spang-dab into the goddamn cuspidor."

The Professor was on his feet, his face an impotent frenzy.

"I reckon you gonna have t'haul it out of there, Professor; it ain't like me to go fishin' in spittoons."

The pack, as though some hand had suddenly dropped all the leashes at once, exploded in the gushing roar that brought down rocks and tore caverns into the earth. And Og, the explosion and a thousand others echoing inside his head, stepped forward. He grasped the book that protruded from the cuspidor, lifted it, brown strings of spittle trailing, and laid it on the bar. Beanpod's face hung directly over him. A sudden silence seized the group.

Then, through the mouth that had difficulty making words when the pressure of sound was upon it, Og's voice came, echoing the blast.

"No more laughin' . . . no more . . . no more laughin' . . ."

Og thrust his face upward. Beanpod backed away a step and Og followed. Then Beanpod seemed to freeze, overpowered and witless, staring with some sort of passion into the face some three inches below his own. His right hand dropped toward the revolver in his belt scabbard.

Og's knife darted up like a small bird flushed from hiding and stuck under the big, square chin. Beanpod dropped to the floor with a squawk. The group behind began to break into shreds. Several backed out of range of the knife thrust and attempted to regroup in some kind of orderly line. A sprinkling of revolvers showed at waistlines. Og tossed his knife and caught it in his palm, handle forward, in throwing position. There were no more reachings. The faces were puzzled, frightened, grim. At last a voice sounded from among them:

"We was funnin', friend. No hurt in fellers havin' some fun. We don't mean no hurt to no one, and it weren't very nice of you to stick Jack there with your knife thataway."

Og could not tell from which precise spot in the line the whining voice was coming from, for he had fixed the whole of it with his eye, not noticing that the small cluster had already begun to fall apart. It continued to dissolve as he stared: one by one its pieces dropped quietly away, each making a wide circle around Og and out the double doors. Beanpod, who had finally worked himself to his hands and knees and was spitting into a growing stain on the floor, at last heaved to his feet and bolted toward daylight, leaving his hat, a dented black fragment of himself, beside the spreading watered spot of his blood.

The Professor had sat through it stunned, much as he had been on that other day when Beanpod had popped the cap with the revolver pointed at his head. Og picked up the book by its dry edge, walked over and laid it down in front of the Professor, and took the chair at the table opposite him. The Professor looked at the brown-soaked pages and shook his head.

"Read it to me," said Og. He was scarcely amazed to hear the plea in his voice.

The Professor continued to shake his head. For a long time he sat in a silence of his own which Og, who well understood such solitary silences, could not penetrate. Finally the Professor spoke.

"It's your doing." He shook his head again, staring at the ruined book.

"Read to me," Og repeated.

The Professor's head still moved slowly to and fro as he looked into the book in front of him.

"You had no right," he said. "As the man said, it was not for you to interfere and stop it all. . . . They did nothing that I did not of my own will permit them to do. I was beginning to know them and to make myself known to them. Even ridicule is a form of understanding between men; but you misunderstood. . . . How could you understand? You, who so obviously are not a part of the body of mankind. I was beginning to reach them. They were beginning to accept me as one of them, and only by being one of them could I fulfill my mission of teaching them — of bringing them to the grace of civilization, of all the blessings of the progress of mankind. I had never been able to realize my goal of being one of them, but I was on the brink of doing so. . . . You have spoiled it."

Og listened and could not stop his own words from forming; they rushed out: "I got a mine . . . " and started over. "I got a cabin off south in the canyon country . . . maybe get me some chickens, maybe a sow," and he heard clearly the impediment his twisted face gave the words.

"I saved," the Professor was saying separately. "I accumulated a small fortune, you might say, in order to come out here to fulfill a mission of my own assignment. Now you have ended a dream."

"I don't want no money," Og tried to answer, although the Professor, staring far into the opposite wall, had seemed not to be talking to him. "I got a mine," Og continued, "richest copper ore anyone's ever dug out in these parts. I got a cabin, new team, wagon,

maybe buy me some furniture, few head of cattle . . . "
Worst of all, Og did not know himself — neither the self that babbled onward now nor the one, equally a stranger, who had left the canyon three days ago.

The Professor turned to face Og. "But you only meant to be kind," he said quietly. "Now I'll buy a bottle for the two of us. I've bought none these many months; I've let *them* buy the bottles." He motioned to the bartender, who was standing back from the far side of the bar, still holding the crusted little shotgun he had snatched from some hiding place during the height of the fracas; he grinned with relief under a hanging mustache, slipped the nostrilled piece back under the bar, and came forward with a bottle and two glasses.

"I've let them buy the bottles, after they've had their amusement with me. It was shameful, in a manner of speaking, but I perceived it as a means to my ultimate end: allowing them to buy me the drinks was a means to instilling in them a certain confidence that furthered my ends. I shan't burden you with these details; because of your misguided actions they are no longer of consequence."

The Professor seized the bottle by the neck as soon as the bartender set it down. He drew it to him with a jerk, but having a second thought he poured a little in Og's glass first. Then he poured himself a stiff one and gulped it. He sat a moment, awaiting the certain effect.

"I have not talked thus to a man in many a month," he continued, "and perhaps I should regard it as the beginning of something, rather than an ending." He tipped the bottle and measured another generous drink.

"Perhaps," said the Professor after he had emptied his glass again, "it is I who should be grateful to you, for I take it that you are inviting me to join your enterprise. I have never worked with my hands, yet I seek community with those who do. Perhaps this is my true area of neglect, and perhaps, if you are indeed willing to have me, I shall come with you. You will not find me a competent worker, but I have my savings to contribute to the venture. I shall apprentice myself to you, friend. I shall experience the virtues of productive labor, which shall be its own reward. I must take my books and I must read; I shall request that you listen to me read aloud at times. This is all that I require. Otherwise I shall respect your seniority and place my resources at your disposal. Yes, it's settled . . . you will share my poor lodgings tonight, and on the morrow I shall accompany you."

In the morning, the Professor rolled together the few possessions he had seen fit to bring with him to this unlikely place, packed his many books into the boxes from which he had scarcely unpacked them, and threw everything onto Og's wagon. On the board walks, on the rutted spaces between the buildings, a scattered few morning faces watched after them as the wagon shrunk away from the wide street of the town onto the road that wound off into the wilderness; and one of the faces, a black one, watched longer than the others — watched until the wagon disappeared around the last bend on the familiar road to the valley, the cabin, and the mine.

When the wagon had finally disappeared, Dot turned away, shook his head and grinned. He turned and walked into the loan shop and laid his cloth sack on the counter. The shrunken, ageless man snatched it up and forced his spiny fingers into the drawstring mouth.

"Count it," said Dot. "They's coin enough there to pay for that banjo. I'll be takin' it along with me now."

8

THE TOWNSPEOPLE AND THOSE from the hinterland who frequented the town talked of the Professor for many weeks after he had left; they laughed, because their laughter had been a part of his being, but they spoke of him with gentle mockery and something like respect. For all his crazy talk and reading, they were forced to admit he had a brain — addled, perhaps, but brilliant. He might even have been somebody once. Maybe the trouble was a woman, maybe the booze.

But the Professor, distant and different as he was, had surely once been among them, if not really one of them. He had gone off with a hardly believable man who didn't look like a man at all; had no face, yet face enough to make a right and common man turn from it — and man enough to fight and kill anything, man or beast, give any odds, no kind of creature to fool with; yet the Professor had gone . . .

Thus the talk turned to Og Jenks, another among them yet apart, who provided another sort of diversion. The older talk of Og Jenks, the chill and sober tales, some old as settlement, presented a rich background for the new (" . . . and the way he stuck him with that knife, quicker'n a man can draw, and just for hoorawin' the Professor."). And the tales and their turning wove themselves into the fixed fiber of the formless, unjustified community itself, floating, undisciplined, changing as one of its clouds.

But talk inevitably faded as the town drifted another two or three months in time; the old tales blended with the new and finally thinned to an occasional, "Remember the Professor . . . ?" giving way to such solid stuff as the new connecting railroad, talk of which had already nearly put the Stage Line out of business: talk, in the end the strongest force on that fluid frontier.

Then the return of the Professor in the flesh suddenly put him deeper in the core of the town's interest than he had ever been and added a new mystery, far more stimulating than the one that had been the Professor himself.

Summer had not entirely given out, but the town and the higher country had already known a spell of winter, now evaporating in the wind and soaking the clay street to mud. The Professor rode in, as a manner of speaking: he was on the back of a horse, but his head hung low over the pommel and his body balanced in the saddle like a sack of grain, flowing to and fro within its tight skin with the motions of the horse. Each time a hoof failed to find its place in the deceptive mud it seemed that the body would topple to the street, yet it somehow kept its place, and for how many miles it had maintained such a posture nobody could guess.

Drunk? He obviously was not, but that question had to be asked and answered first. Sick.

They lifted him from the saddle and carried him to his old room which had remained unoccupied and probably would have for all time to come — only now the Professor was back. Somebody built a fire in the cold, sooty little stove. Somebody else called in Doc

Byers. In an instant the apathetic town was busy as a new hive.

Pneumonia, the doctor said; he had a high fever, and pneumonia was bad in the thin air of the high country, especially in a man with the Professor's delicate frame. The Professor was out of his head and raving, and the townspeople, in spite of their solicitude, were more interested in his rambling words than in the doctor's. But the doctor sent them all home, saying the Professor was done, that the end was certain sometime before dawn, probably in the small hours — the favored time for pneumonia to claim its own.

Deep into the evening the Professor dropped into a coma and the doctor made him as comfortable as he should and left him. In the morning he returned, expecting to call somebody to carry out the corpse, call some unofficial public servant to open a grave on the unwanted land beyond the limits of settlement, and to write out a death certificate; he found the Professor lying as he had left him, not in the wax-gray film of a corpse, but in a resting, easy-breathing sleep, a living color in his face.

Doc Byers was an old man, bringing the old wisdom of experience to a young country to be used up in the expending vitality, but he had little of what the profession would come to call, in its glib years of maturity, formal training — no medical school certificate and none of the written and learned laws of physiology and the related sciences with which to express meaningfully that which he did not understand; so he merely scratched his chin, shook his head, and went about doing such things as he had always considered proper to do for a recovering pneumonia patient, that which his godless mind had secretly come to call "the healing power" having, as always, performed the principal task. He was as sure now that the Professor would recover as he had been the night before that he would not.

A few days later the Professor was sitting up in bed, talking rationally and drinking the whiskey he had been brought. The one change from his former life in the town was that he was now receiving visitors in his own living quarters. And visitors, many of them seeing the Professor's room for the first time and labeling it appropriately a "boar's nest," kept on coming. They came to listen and drink and explore — to gain material for talk that would go on in many places, for many months; but they came also out of curiosity: to see the man who had returned, first from Og Jenks and the forbidding canyon country out south, then from the dead. The old mystery of the Professor himself had ceased to be the primary one; the single question in everybody's mind was, What happened between the two of them down there?

Since the fever left him, the Professor seemed not to want to talk about it, but little by little a sketchy, hardly adequate story was put together from the pieces he reluctantly let drop. Not long after the Professor had moved in, Og's early cheerfulness wore thin; he became less talkative, more surly. His impatience grew at the Professor's physical ineptitude during work at the mine; he grumbled and muttered wordlessly through the evenings as the Professor sat with his books, and when the Professor read aloud, as was his habit whether anyone were listening or not, Og would stomp out of the cabin. He told the Professor he was drinking too much and sleeping too late in the mornings, and he took the supply of whiskey out and smashed the bottles on the slag pile. Then, on the final evening . . .

"I couldn't think," said the Professor, his voice

breaking, stammering into the memory. "My head was empty. All I saw was him dropping my book into the stove, then myself hurling books at him from the pile beside my bed, one after another. I had become as he. I at last was something he could understand, for he took out that ugly knife and charged at me, chased me around the room and out the door. I stood long, knocking at the door to get back in and recover my money and my possessions, even my clothing. But he would not open. There was thus nothing for me to do but make my way back to town."

What more was there to it? Must be something. . . . Talk embellished the story, framed it out. But before the Professor was quite ready to leave his bed, the people of the town got half an answer to the puzzle. Late one afternoon Og Jenks rolled down the street high on the seat of his big spring wagon. He went to the bar and had a drink or two — alone as usual, and listening and alert. He stayed until nearly sundown, then he left the saloon, crossed the street and disappeared into the alley beside the drygoods store where the Professor had his room.

In a few minutes came shouts and a white figure waving like a tall flag in the broad dusk. It was the Professor, in his nightshirt and running, weaving on spindly legs — but he didn't run far. The next instant a small crowd had gathered around him; two men had taken hold of him and his shouts faded to wayward mutterings. The town marshal and two of the more curious retraced the Professor's steps toward his room, and there in the alley by the store in the shadows was Og Jenks. The marshal and the two followers studied what they could see in the darkness of the bent, changeless face. Og, too, was muttering:

"Stole my horse, just come back to get the horse he stole from me when he run out of my place, and he comes undone — throws a half-full bedpot across the room at my head . . . screams, rants . . . "

The marshal and his two self-appointed deputies looked at one another. Horse thievery: that was something they understood readily and condemned without deliberation. There was, of course, the Professor's talk about Og keeping in his cabin all his possessions, his books, burning one and maybe all the rest of them. That, in its way, was thievery. But horse stealing? Og was clearly within his rights in trailing a horse thief and coming to claim his own property. But there stood Og, and the Good Lord only knew what he might do next. A lawman couldn't leave things this way; he exchanged further glances with his companions.

"Drunk," said the marshal finally, with spirit. The other two grinned and nodded their agreement. "Drunk." The marshal took a cautious step toward Og. "Come on with me, Mister Jenks, I got your hotel ready over there. Come along and take a little nap; you'll feel fit as can be in the morning." Then with one of the quick and skillful movements that explained his survival over the years in his profession, the marshal snatched Og's knife from the shirt scabbard. Disarmed, Og dropped his head, hiding his face, and let the marshal lead him off to jail. The Professor was led by charitable hands back to his room.

The brief activity in the street would have made material for a new turn in the town's talk, but the time for assembling, conjecturing, arguments and rebuttals was never allowed. Hardly had the town settled down for the first chewings, the story began its making again. This time it was at the jail, where the marshal dozing in a chair in his office was suddenly awakened by what he, in twenty years of keeping the law, could never have mistaken for anything but a rifle shot, and close by.

He rushed outside, waking up on the way, around the little low building. There, under the cell window, standing beside an upturned box with a rifle tucked under his arm, was the Professor. Greasy black powder smudged the front of his nightshirt, and the smell of it hung around him. The old Sharps was slipping slowly from his loosening grip.

The marshal took the Professor by the arm, slipped the old carbine from under his other arm, and hurried him inside the office. On his way, he peered through the bars and saw Og, his single eye wide, sitting up on the cell bunk. There was only one cell and the marshal had to make a decision. He opened the door and ordered Og out; then he gently eased the Professor into the cell and turned the key. Og walked out onto the street without a word. Later, when the marshal tried to find him to ask him some questions about the matter, he was told that Og had taken his team and wagon and quietly left town.

Now the marshal himself propelled the talk: "Climbed up on a box, he did, and stuck the barrel between the bars, but his eyesight was bad and so was that old Sharps and it was black inside that cell, and what looked to be Og layin' there weren't. So we just got ourselves a mashed rifle ball stuck in the mortar between the brick."

And the Professor, when he was able to talk again, gasped for words: "Three times now . . . I, a dedicated man of peace, have resorted to . . . violence because of the evil of that man which has infected me like a disease. I was certain he would kill me when he was released from jail, he threatened as much, clearly. . . . That old firearm . . . it has leaned against the wall of my room since I moved in. I don't know where it came from, nor did I ever dream of taking such an instrument of death into my hands, yet . . . I have become as he . . . By fighting savagery, I have become a savage . . . lost to civilized man . . . yet, somehow I must return. How can I?"

And from that night and for many days and nights to come the town was split over the affair. Og Jenks and the Professor never by their very nature having been of the flesh of the town, the people could argue and debate it as an event in some far fixed point in history or the Bible or such other sources as embraced figures formed in printed words or the imagery of artists: horse thievery, book thievery, bedpots, knives, rifles; Og Jenks and the Professor performing as if in a puppet theater set up in the middle of the wide, dusty street. Og Jenks had disappeared from the town, not to be seen for many months; and the Professor, strangely defeated by the whole episode, never spoke of it again — indeed, spoke little of anything from that day on, his silence deepening both the older mystery of himself and the mystery of the affair of Og Jenks. The town went on guessing. They were still guessing when the circuit judge came and sat and took the Professor's guilty plea and sentenced him for attempted murder and assault with a deadly weapon.

The talk continued after they hauled the Professor away in the closed, horse-drawn wagon, Og Jenks down working whatever it was he called a mine in a country nobody cared to venture into; it continued with the town finally emptied of both of them. If there were more to it than had been discovered, if there were such a thing as a final truth, who was there to tell it? Could anybody imagine Og Jenks coming before them and telling the story? And the Professor. He died three months after he entered the territorial prison: exact age, unknown; birthplace, unknown; next of kin, unknown.

9

Og jenks's third partnership grew out of a time, a place and a practical need.

The smiling young Texan went by the name of Huston, without the "o," and that was the only name, first or last, that was ever attached to him in that foreign land into which he had wandered. Og met him on the trail leading down from the high plateau where a railroad construction camp was located, and the two of them had at that moment a common need and a common obstacle. The need was money and the obstacle was winter.

Og had money, a good sum, in the tin box under the floorboard of his cabin; but the amount was perhaps a thousandth of that represented by the ore still in its pocket in the mine. He had found that he must have more cash in hand if he were to get all the mine held, and this he had finally and above all become determined to do. He had no more notion than ever of what he might do with the wealth, but the mine was withholding it from him — deepening, twisting and in need of shoring, and blasting had become tricky. He must get the ore away from the mine, and all of it and by himself.

Og had allowed an image to begin forming of himself standing before a banker, pleading for a loan, but he turned abruptly away from it before it was fully formed. It was a poor time of year for any kind of stealing. Although he lived in a time and place wherein nearly every man, according to his need and ability, stole at some time in his life, Og had never done it. The refraining had little to do with scruples; it was more through contempt for anything owned and cherished by another and coveted by many.

Then Og recalled that during one of his days in the saloon where words drifted freely and aimlessly as indoor dust he had overheard something about one of the men for whom he had once worked: an official of the Stage Line, as he recalled the fragment, was in some overseeing position in the construction of the new connecting railroad that was to run along the old stagecoach route. He was a man with whom Og knew he could deal, and it was worth a trip. Og found him in a makeshift shack heated by a tin-box stove, the headquarters for the dreary construction camp which was about to be closed for the season by the wind and snow of that short-sagebrush country. It was thus that Og was awarded a contract to supply the camp with tie-timbers for the next season's construction, and he signed the contract on the boldest of nerve: it called for more than any one man could possibly supply in the time allowed. Og lied. He told them he had a helper. Nor did he tell them that he planned to go far beyond what the contract called for and supply himself with mine timbers; so despite two distasteful experiences, Og Jenks found himself looking for another . . . but he had told the railroad work boss it was a helper he had, so a helper he was seeking, not a partner. The simple change of words made the prospect less forbidding. He had become well accustomed to it when a few miles' ride out of the railroad camp Huston turned up.

Huston was scarcely more than a boy, but roughly used by weather, hard work, and the essential cruelty involved in the process of living and staying alive. Yet not the slightest shade of cruelty crossed his face. He was well made in feature and limb, tall and very slender, but wiry with heavy wrists and big, thick-skinned hands. He was a drover who had come with one of the herds that had started to trickle in from Texas a few years back and were now flowing like a river during the milder months with this later talk of more railroads and growing proof that cattle could well withstand what had once been considered winters barely fit for man and totally unfit for beast. Some of the stockmen were also beginning to discover the gentle winters of the lower country and more and more to consider them an expedient rather than a mere curiosity of nature. More and more cattle were being wintered in the mild bottoms of the canyons, closer and ever closer to Og's valley.

The herd with which Huston had come north had been sold as contracted and the drovers paid off. Huston, boylike, had sought to parlay his roll into something more than a mere stake back to Texas for another spring and another herd, another boss and another drudging drive with its hate and humiliation, then another payroll; he had lost it all to the shrewd bone-picking faces under the hard derby hats. Outwardly he was disgruntled and remorseful; inwardly he was downright frightened. He had never been outside the county of his birthplace in Texas before he joined the drive, and he looked to the coming winter, about which he had heard the lavish and overdrawn tales, with the dread of a child newly orphaned.

At the time he met Og, Huston was on his way to the railroad camp to ask for work — anything to make a few dollars to fill his saddlebags and get back to warm, secure Texas. Only a few words of persuasion from Og, and Huston had turned his horse around and was riding south (possibly ten, twenty miles closer to Texas anyway) with his new employer. Within their first few minutes of riding together Huston had told Og his whole distressed story and Og had convinced him that this job of tie-cutting for the new railroad was probably the only paying job in the country this season, with the railroad laying off for the winter, a panic on back in the states and all. Then Og with his new skill at making words, drawn through the skins of his first two partners, added a few to shrink the inflated tales of winter that were haunting Huston and spoke of making camp a few miles down below where water was flowing and leaves were unseared by the plateau winds, of cooking up the food in his saddlebags, and plenty for two.

The young, despairing drover seemed to embrace the very ugliness of Og with his two eyes; he seemed, in fact, to have noticed in that moment for the first time the undone face. Og saw the glance, saw compassion in the proud young eyes and was filled with hatred; but he had a practical need and he knew that compassion could be made to pay.

That night, clear and cold and still with no hint of snow, they made their camp in the timber and Og rode back south to his canyon to fetch back the wagon and team and supplies. Late the following day he returned and Huston began transforming his gratitude and his charitable feelings into hard work for Og. He was strong and energetic, he was skillful with the double-bitted ax or wedge and he was untiring on one end of the crosscut saw. He talked little while he worked, but in the evening he told Og about being born on a timbered East Texas farm, born and grown to boyhood before the farm was half cleared and so was born, as he put it, on one end of a saw. In the days that followed he proved it, working from dark morning to dark evening on the meager rations Og doled out to both of them, and he seemed nearly happy, as though the work itself recalled a childhood he had left under protest. Worse for Og, he eventually grew cheerful, even as Og grew more sullen — made himself poor company and an irascible employer and tightened even harder on the food. Snow came and Huston laughed with it. Snow piled a foot deep around the flapping canvas of their tent, and more piled on top of it. Huston laughed louder and talked of spring.

Then the worst of the winter came and the trees had to be cut high on their trunks at the snowline so that the heaviest and best of the timber was lost. For several days blizzard thickened the air so that work was out of the question, and the two of them huddled in the tent over a makeshift tincan stove, going out only to hay and grain the horses. Og cursed these days silently, even to the horses that ate costly feed and gave no return. He thought of his cabin in the mild shelter of the canyon in the lower country where snow seldom stayed (take your damn Texas, you young whelp, and take your talk too), and Huston talked; seeing Og's gloom, his compassion rose, then seeing Og's face his young heart seemed to suffer until Og, suffering in his own way, longed to tunnel into a snowbank to wait out the storm. He wanted to say aloud, I live with my face, try living with your own; but he only reminded himself that he still had a need, that only a few weeks more and the quota of railroad ties would be filled and he could press Huston on for mine timbers. Beyond this he wasn't thinking, only waiting.

Wind would come, then sun; snow would shrink, then crust — a floor for the next storm to walk across; but between there were bright days, some so warm that coats were shed over the sweating saw and ax. On these days there began to be long dawdling pauses in Huston's work, and often he gazed with hands at rest into the gloomy snowbound forest and toward the bright opening where the river stood in its icy grip between the black and white wooded banks. It might have been spring already in Texas; by the calculation of any man who cared to calculate it probably was. Huston seemed to sniff at new wet earth and mesquite, sensing the passing of the final frost and budding down below the Red River where all mesquite and all Texas and all springtime began. Sometimes it seemed he was ready to question . . . the huge piles of timbers cut to lengths and neatly stacked to represent pay for honest work, the long days and the endless work in the prison of winter with never a mention of time running close to ending, never a mention of pay. Huston never questioned, not aloud; but his gaiety and good spirit had faded with his suncolor to a pale sullenness, not unlike the mood in which Og had first found him.

The anger, the brooding questions lay deep, Og understood, and he knew they must sometime be voiced and in some manner answered . . . when? Og wondered, and how soon? When must the mood Og had almost deliberately created in the man be turned inside out, and what would then be the expedient thing for Og to do? Og had always had immense faith in the decisions given to be known on the brink of action, but now he tended against his better judgment to ponder and plot. Mild and congenial as Huston had been, he had lived on payday and Texas through these dreary mountain months, and Og could hardly see it an easy matter to part with Huston without

Huston getting his due. It had even occurred to Og often that he might pay Huston off and make an easy thing of it, but the consideration violated something deep and mysterious and tender in Og, and he was forced each time to set it aside. In the end he fell back on his old faith that the proper course would be taken at the proper time, with no hint of what or when beforehand. He would collect what was due him under the contract because a company must make good. But a company was not a man — most certainly not an Ogden Jenks.

Always cautious, Og had grown even more so over the years as the realization of himself in terms of wealth and property grew. He had noticed with care, for instance, that Huston was never without his revolver. This was, he understood, partly because a gun was to this man from Texas a deeply personal symbol, much as was a big gold watch to a railroad engineer. Also, Huston took a certain toying delight in the big-blunt-butted weapon with its slim barrel and powerful, perfectly timed springs. He had once demonstrated it to Og with ritual, without, however, letting it leave his own hand; he had explained that it was one of the new Peacemakers and one of the first turned out of Colt's factory back East just last year, that he had traded for it, apparently with sentimental reluctance, his daddy's old Navy Colt, even though the Navy had just been drilled out to take the new brass cartridges.

And when it wasn't a plaything, the Peacemaker was a comforting companion and a tool to Huston the newly grown man. Huston scorned a rifle as Og scorned all firearms, and on milder days he would sometimes take a stroll around sundown and always come back demonstratively with meat for the camp, whether a grouse with its head shot off clean or a small tender deer with a hole dead center through its heart. At such times Og had considered the saving in supplies bought out of his own pocket and was quietly grateful to the revolver and to Huston's skill. Now, as the season lengthened, both had to be considered; for with a mere notion of spring in the high-country forest a deep slow change was coming over Huston, like sap rising in a plant at a given time, even with the plant far removed from its native climate. Og knew the turning would come, and with all his concern he went on watching and waiting with the patience of that better time of his life when little or nothing mattered.

The proper time was long in the making and came, as Og had known it would, in a single instant as he stood on the bank of the frozen river, blown clean of snow by a recent wind. Huston had crossed to gather dry firewood, long since cleaned up in the vicinity of the camp, and now he was recrossing the broad frozen slab, arms piled with a tangle of boughs and pitch-laden chunks of pine stump; he stepped carefully, feeling his balance as he put one heeled foot in front of the other, his body weaving and twisting but faithfully clinging to the fuel for their fire. Thoughts, even feelings, rushed into Og's head but he swept them away, swept his brain blank as he had learned to do some-time before memory began; he stepped out on the ice with his flat, heavy, hobnailed lace boots, the footgear of common sense compared with the contemptible things into which Huston thrust his feet every morn-ing. He met Huston in the middle of the river, the two of them surrounded by the acres of water arrested in flow by the quick and durable subzero cold these many weeks, and he extended his hand toward a crooked, clamping elbow embracing the firewood. He offered a rare word, too: "Slick, ain't it? Wind's swept the snow off clean," and Huston faltered, caught him-self and grinned. "Here, let me help you along in them heels," and Og fixed his own balance firmly and reached farther.

He wrapped an ungloved hand around Huston's load-bent right wrist and stepped to one side, assuming an effective position to guide him on the rest of the walk over the ice to the low bank where the flat-trodden snow path led a few feet to the camp . . . an effective position too for raising a knee quickly to catch Huston in the back of the thigh, action completed, firewood scattered in many directions, skidding and twisting as it alighted like so many blown leaves on the surface of the river; but Huston didn't fall. He had recovered himself remarkably on his absurd boots and now stood facing Og, no questions, no bewilderment, not even dismay or anger in his eyes, for he too, as it was turning out, was a man who had learned well to act in a moment of action and think in a moment of thought.

Huston's right glove had gone with the wood, and somehow the revolver had come into the bare, glove-warm hand; but his heel had slipped a trace and the shot went wild and free as the little sounds it set erupting among the trees. Huston's thumb was returning the hammer to cock as the gun bounced off its own recoil and Og's knife drew a quick arc and severed the holding wrist tendons and the hammer fell. The gun exploded again as it dropped like an unstrung puppet to the ice while Og drove his knife forward and drove it again. Huston doubled over and fell in a jackknife heap. Og was on him like a small wrestling boy and was working his knife in short strokes; when Og stood up again he had cut all trace of life out of his third partner, as he could now let himself call him.

Og stood straight, head bowed and huge eye taking in the task just performed. He stood a long time, until his emptied mind began slowly to fill again.

Bury him? Where in this frozen ground? Might as well try to sink a pick or shovel into a pig of iron.

There was timber, several loads of it to be hauled to the railroad construction camp as soon as the snow was melted enough to let him make his way with the team down the slope in the spring mud. After the payoff from the railroad there were more timbers to be taken to the mine, then the drills again, and the dynamite and the ore — the ore, the vein of ore that had now as good as lost its fight to stay in its ancient place under the hill. The mine would be conquered, mined out and dead, a dead worthless hole and Og would be free again, with nothing the world wanted, the world having nothing he needed.

He could leave this thing, this slashed up bundle of rags thrust out of his being now and into a past that may as well never have existed, leave it right here on the ice for the real and faithful future to take care of . . . this ice that would be no more in weeks, perhaps even days, when the river would explode like gunshots, resume its flow where it had been fixed in sudden sleep, push the demolished ice along into the thunder of spring and white water, and take this business, this dissolved partnership of Og's, with it down into the canyon country, to greater rivers and the wild rapids in the junctions where the smallest bits of wood were ground to still smaller bits.

When Og at last turned his back on it and walked to the bank and camp, the matter was closed to him; had he known that what he had envisioned and what really happened were not quite the same, it would have been of little consequence to him. He did not know because, when the party of geologists came through that way about two weeks later with Og's first partner, who had hired on as cook, Og had long since worked his way down the slope with the first load of ties. The party had ventured too high too early in the season, but their leader, a stubborn man, had gone against all the unscientific wisdom, all the warnings of Dot and others who lived with and against the country. He was a professor from an eastern university who had hired out to the Geological Survey during a sabbatical leave, working under contract to the government to make geological maps and at the same time writing a monograph on the Laramide Revolution.

The professor, a little in the lead of the party, was the first to notice a dark mass out on the frozen river, and with pedantic curiosity he dismounted and walked out over the ice to investigate. Dot, just a little way behind, had passed through the leavings of the camp and seen the remainder of the stacked timbers. He got down off his mule and followed the professor out on the ice.

"He didn't die naturally." The professor was standing over the frosted corpse lying among the scattered pieces of brittle firewood. The professor shook his head and his mouth twitched. "This poor chap's met with foul play, and it was no wild beast. See? There lies his revolver, which he obviously tried to use."

Dot stood beside him, somehow less horrified by the sight than the professor. He kept glancing back toward the abandoned campsite. Then another of the party, catching up, walked on the ice to join them and stare, his face frozen as that of the corpse.

"Well, we can't possibly bury him in this frozen ground, but at least we can take the body to some appropriate place, gather some rocks and build a cairn. Come on . . ." The professor seemed to weaken; he turned away, a shudder in his voice. "Horrible. I wonder who, or what . . ."

"A bad man, a natural all-bad man I guess most folks would name him. Me, I ain't namin' him none."

105

The professor turned to his cook: "You mean you know who . . . ? What manner of country is this?"

"Ain't namin' the way of the country, neither," Dot answered, "and I can't hardly name the way of the man. . . . Know him? I spose. The way that there cut-up dead man know him. But somehow that ain't hardly knowin'."

10

A FILM OF CIVILIZATION GREW THIN, in slowly spreading specks, like sickly mold on the vast landscape, but for many years none of its spores blew into the valley and its canyons where Og lived and mined. The valley remained far from the tenuous grasp of white man's law — a retreat for those who lived off the scant wealth of virgin land: the cattle and horse thieves, the petty thieves, the genial robbers of trains, mine payrolls, banks. They came and went, up and down the oblique highway marked only for their eyes, with the valley as its midpoint.

Og kept inching his tunnel deeper into the hillside, drifting up toward the heart of the copper vein; the ore, richer day by day, fell to the dynamite blasts; the slag pile grew outward, sliding down and befouling the creek, flattening at the mouth of the tunnel until it became a broad and convenient platform for grading the ore, for halting, loading, and turning the wagon. Og worked on toward no day or goal. From time to time the crude roof of his cabin would spring a leak, and if the leak were not directly over his bed or the stove, if it were not the season of small afternoon summer rains or melting snows, he would let it go unrepaired until finally compelled to take his ax and shave shingles from a cedar firewood log to shut out the weather.

And during the days and seasons that Og worked deep in his mine, out in the broad sunlight of the valley several squat log cabins with split-rail corrals half hidden in tall sagebrush had made their tiny intrusions on the great flat expanse between the rising rock walls, barely visible specks from the turn at the top of the road leading out of Og's canyon. Sometimes a small herd of cattle would appear, like a flung fistful of seed, spread over the flat river bottom and upward onto the slopes, less noticeable, except for occasional faraway bawling, than a grazing band of antelope still fearlessly occupying their place of centuries. But the cattle came and went: they were probably stolen and hidden in the valley until a proper market could be found. Not really intrusion: neither the people nor the cattle were numerous enough or close enough to threaten Og's solitude.

Occasionally, as Og made the old turn up into the canyon, he came briefly into the distant view of a black man with two mules loaded with camp supplies and mining tools. Dot, wherever he might choose to go to spend a month or a season, wherever his needs might take him, usually found himself wandering again into the valley to enjoy there the strange homeness he felt in no other place. And unlike Og, he saw and marked each small change in the valley's face: the dirt-floor cabins grown short out of the ground — a roof over someone's head; a floor and a new room in the cabin; a woman, a child, a home.

Scratching at the steep valley walls and poking into the side canyons, Dot sometimes panned a few dollars worth of gold from one of the many streams that fed the river, but never enough to make it worthwhile to set up a sluice box. Once or twice he dug out a few chunks of lead carbonate that could possibly have held some silver, but it was of too low a grade to be worth taking in for assay. The small discoveries, small events in the bigness of the land and of his life he strung into talk and gave it, like the measures of corn and oats from the sacks, to his mules. But for the big joy, the joy of the search, he turned to the rich and appropriate language of his banjo and the songs he made for it.

As Og's copper ore richened and the loads that could profitably be shipped to the custom smelter became smaller, his trips into town became more frequent. He worked through days that flowed into one another in unmarked stream, and abruptly another pile of high-grade ore would appear at the mouth of the mine; he would load up and go, spend his two days in town and return with supplies and a fat money pouch. Sometimes in the evenings, allowing himself an hour or so before blowing out the lamp to save the supply of coal-oil, he would get out his tin box and count, then stack and grade the coin like ore, until this single, small amusement wore thin in the orange lamplight.

Though Og took no notice of it, the town, centered on its million square miles of mountains, plateaus, deserts and high plains, had changed. Situated on the nation's first east-west railway and in the northward thrust of the burgeoning beef industry, it responded to the successive intrusions: new railroads ate wide miles of land on either side of their slender roadbeds, and the speculators came; settlers followed to repeat the pattern of clearing, building, fencing and plowing, and ran up against an enemy unknown to their fathers and grandfathers — bigness. Then the government began giving away 160-acre parcels of land to any family that could prove itself worthy, and the land was divided: less land per family, more families per square mile, more people, more products, more bought and sold, more homes, more . . .

Costumes changed: the fringe vanished from the buckskin, then the buckskin vanished, and faces clean-shaven in admiration of the Indians' grew beards. There was talk of a three-story hotel in town, of new shipping pens for cattle at the railroad, of a kiln to make brick for a proper sort of building, of a sawmill to devour the timber off the slopes where grass would then grow to feed next summer's trail herds, twice the size of last summer's, out of the south. . . .

Still, the town, its sleepy, secure isolation being chipped away from it bit by bit, held fast to that which belonged to its past and present: its own talk, its own tales, the making of its own legends. The town, where the overland trail went over the pass in the long wrinkle of stunted mountains, had formerly been a stopping place for the wagons, the people passing through with no concern for the big country except as a cursed barrier to the land beyond and the other ocean; later it became a place where the shrill loco-motives, overloaded with cars and panting up the gentle slope, took on wood and water. The town had survived smugly its own accidental beginnings; now it had begun very nearly to thrive.

When Og Jenks married Marcel Jones, it was an event that touched, warmed and entertained every segment and level of the town for a few heady hours. The townspeople were more than ready for some such binding force. Reaching out of undirected instinct for self-realization as a community, they needed something from time to time — anything larger than the spon-taneous process of town-growth and their own circum-

110

scribed lives — to provide some transcendent emotion. And this was what the marriage of Og and Marcel accomplished.

The circumstances building toward the event were not too different from those that occasioned the mail-order marriages that abounded in that part of the country. A man through some effort and luck would find himself in a position to support a woman, and, no woman being available, he resorted with no loss of esteem (certainly not the loss that becoming a squaw-man would have meant) to advertising. But the arrangement of Og Jenks's marriage lacked even the privacy of the public mails.

Og had long since come to be one of the properties of the town — external to its life, rarely seen and almost entirely unknown in the community sense of "knowing"; yet, like the curious standing rock formation nearby that the Indians said was a woman turned to stone for being unfaithful to her husband, he was one of the area's natural phenomena, unfailingly described or pointed out to visitor and newcomer. Bad, mean, evil, dangerous? Og was beyond such words. The things he had done, and the many things he had never done were well known. Nobody judged them. It was Og Jenks who did them and that was the judgment. Had it been a man more of the flesh of the community, a whole man with a whole face, real and solid and touchable who could speak and be spoken to with ease, he might have been hanged or banished, but Og Jenks . . . ? Nobody knew. When he didn't show up in town for months at a time, which had often been the case in the past, people seemed inclined to doubt that he existed at all. His flesh was the stuff of which talk was made, and talk was all right; but who could have any sympathy for anyone fool enough to get mixed up with him?

Then, quite suddenly and without apparent reason, the talk began to fade and something like a man of real flesh took form in barest outline. Og had taken to coming into town much oftener than usual, sometimes staying as long as three days and an extra night and doing little or no apparent serious business after shipping off his ore, but ingratiating the business people by leaving behind more money than they had ever seen fall from his pockets. That he spent most of it in one place mattered little, since the money had no place to go beyond the town limits and would eventually disseminate to the benefit of all; he spent most of his waking hours in the saloon, never becoming what could be called drunk, but within short hours after his arrival drinking himself into a state of aggravated sociability on remarkably little whiskey, then buying drinks for everybody with a debonair flourish far out of character for the Og of talk and tales. In former days when Og came to town he would speak to no one unless he had business to transact, and then no more than necessary; these days he talked to nearly everybody, though he still managed to keep his words as empty of information about the man within as before. He talked as though blowing froth from some deep agitation.

There had been a time, and only short weeks earlier, that few could say for certain that they had ever heard Og Jenks laugh. There was in fact only one man. This was a stage driver, who used to tell the story often, years back. The driver had broken an axle and had walked on to Og's speck of a station out in the middle of that dust-green desolation. Approaching, he had been stopped frozen in his tracks by a sound he could not even come close to identifying in known nature, yet a sound it seemed he might have heard in some forbidding region of the mind into which he might at

112

some time have ventured. He had gone on cautiously and had at last determined that the sound was coming from Og, who was standing alone in the middle of the corral, his eye fixed on an object propped against the bottom rail. As the driver moved closer, he saw that the object that was entertaining Og so grandly was a pair of wolves hopelessly joined at their rumps. Their own moment past, Og had apparently come upon them in their spent and helpless situation and had killed both of them. He had somehow managed to carry them, still joined, back to his station corral and put them on display against the rail. The sound the driver heard was Og's laughter.

But now, in these days of the frequently-visiting Og, few of the people in the town had not heard his laughter. It had become one of the familiar sounds of the street, day or night, a loud noise rushing from the scar of a mouth in an unbroken blast.

The newly-sociable Og at first met the same cautious response as the Og Jenks of hearsay. Any man he chose to talk to listened, or made a convincing pretense of it. If Og's mangled sounds made the hearer want to laugh, he took care not to show it, for the ugly one and the dangerous unknown were still the only authentic Og Jenks there was. But after a time, traces of amusement began to slip through; and though the scarred face that could not smile looked as menacing as ever, the knife stayed in its shirt scabbard. Men grew bolder. One laughed outright, then another. At last, groups stood around him listening and laughing openly, and the changeless face seemed somehow to join in the laughter. Later still, those who found Og tiresome would readily walk away from him, perhaps to attempt in some other company a passable imitation of the impediment the grotesque face gave to the

113

words. In the end, even an occasional bold jibe failed to arouse the sudden wrath, the swift violence that had been Og Jenks.

There began to be qualms: Had something passed again from them, as had the hostile Indians, the fur trade, the buffalo, the stagecoaches, as other realities of present time were passing into the unreal, dreaming past? Was the legendary Ogden Jenks truly gone? Or had he never really existed except in a few imaginations? Then some pragmatic soul, whose meager portion of imagination had evaporated with childhood, began to diagnose Og's ailment: It wasn't so much what had happened to Og as what had happened all around him — all around everywhere, and to all of them.

Take the lower canyon country down there where Og lived and worked his mine. People were living there now, in what anyone would have to call a civilized manner. Morgan Harris, who for five years had poled a flatboat back and forth across the river and called it a ferry, had made a tidy pile, what with more and more people coming in all the time; he had built a store at his ferry dock and a month later installed the several pigeonholes of a legal United States Post Office behind the cashbox counter, and a man could buy there, under one roof, nearly everything he could buy in town, if he were willing to pay the extra markup and freight. That was progress, by anybody's way of looking at it.

Without ever realizing it, probably, Og had been contributing his share to the development of the valley. Getting the wealth out of the ground where it had been locked over these centuries; why shouldn't he be caught up in it, this change, this moving forward? Why shouldn't he want to have his part in it, along with everybody else?

Nobody could be absolutely, figure-quoting certain, but everybody agreed that Og was a wealthy man by this time, considering the rumored assay of his ore and the number of wagon loads he had hauled to the railroad to be sent to the custom smelter. He must surely have enough to bring . . . at least contentment to . . . But at this point the very real image of Og's face would thrust itself rudely into the cozy visions of the conspirators. Talk, even thought, halted abruptly.

Still, the notion of Og Jenks with woman trouble — the kind that comes from lack of a woman — held possibilities. The people, the town, could not let it stop there. There must be a way . . . something . . . someone . . .

Thus in the space of about a week half a dozen or so townsmen, each believing that the idea was his own, visited Marcel Jones to drop the name of Ogden Jenks. The more trifling ones could only see it all as very funny and had trouble concealing their amusement. Others, with more self-control, had done laughing, and were ready to give the matter a properly serious consideration: Marcel had (they all knew) seen sinful days. But she was good-hearted, despite her past ("Who among us is without blemish?"), and she deserved her own chance in life. And as for Og, all he probably ever needed was to be brought outside himself with a few responsibilities. It was not and never had been good for a man to have no responsibilities in life, never forced to place the consideration of another human being before that of himself. Give him the right sort of home, and the responsibility for keeping it, and he'd be all right.

And if there were any woman in the world who could handle a man like Og, especially with him getting to be a rich man now . . .

On Og's part, without once mentioning the word

"woman" he had done everything but paste up a notice in the postoffice alongside the five-thousand-dollar-reward poster. He had just opened up wide as a mail-order catalog, as they said afterwards when the time came for excusing themselves and washing their hands of the whole thing.

Marcel had known more years than she cared to own, more men than she could possibly recall; yet there was with her always a fixed time of late girlhood which, already stretched far beyond its elastic limits paper-thin and very nearly transparent to the world, was to Marcel still stretching and stretchable; years and men had flocked in and she had tended each one closely to its passing, looking always toward the next, to the discovery that she had yet to acknowledge: that there were fewer both of years and of men in the world, in a single warm skin, than she had ever believed possible.

Yet Marcel was a wise woman, a wisdom of days with a child's capacity to know the present intensely and have only a passing concern for the future — and to keep the past like a told story for retelling: in this respect her wisdom contained no shrewdness, for now in the dwindling days the story of herself, still not real, as was the flesh of her upper arm sagging where it rested on the arm of the chair, embraced the amassing and the passing of two fortunes; and now for the second time in her life she had spent herself into near poverty.

She lived in one room above the dressmaker's shop and cooked on the tiny wood stove that heated the room. During the past year she had taken to sitting through the afternoons at her one window, looking through the crack in the respectable lace curtains out into the street. She wore a shawl that she had crocheted herself and that helped the forming of a new vision of the present — the act of throwing it around her shoulders was like wrapping herself in that vision: the respectable widow behind lace curtains, just turned forty, discreetly waiting and watching.

She had moved into the room right after she had lost the house, when the bank foreclosure could be staved off no longer by words and various persuasions and she was finally forced out the same day and discovered what she had suspected all her life: that women one and all were treacherous hypocrites without a shred of sincerity in all their warmhearted words. Just as soon as it was public knowledge that Marcel was bankrupt, had mortgaged the house and now was being put out on the street practically penniless, not one of the girls would make even a bogus display of sympathy (and one of them had that very evening entertained the president of the bank that foreclosed, no doubt using all the skills that Marcel had so painstakingly encouraged and taught her to develop). Some of the girls, as it came back to her later, had even cursed Marcel for a spendthrift and had more than insinuated that she had come close to getting all of them, along with herself, into financial ruin — Marcel, who had taken every one of them in off the street and given them a home and a place to make a respectable living in proper surroundings. Those . . . and they should be called by their proper biblical designation (although Marcel had never permitted the hateful word to pass her lips) and not "girls," as the patrons called them; they even highhatted her on the street after the foreclosure, and they welcomed the new mistress of the house as a colony of schoolgirls might have welcomed a younger and prettier teacher.

Yet soon it all became part of the story which was to have a very different ending from the one apparent at that time, and the story shifted in the moment from one of the women in Marcel's life to one of the men, for the eternal men were coming to the mean little room into which Marcel had been thrust. She had always known too that men, unlike women, were loyal and just, so long as a girl did not try to possess just one of them and to hone his life and soul down to the size of her own, as did the women who lived according to the will of the Good Lord. Marcel had no natural need for men, and having no such burden she could treat them as objects, as apparent truths, as friends; having no concern for their worldly behavior, she could allow herself to like them — and she genuinely liked them. There was no pretending with a man; a man could be fooled by a woman for a month or a year or maybe a lifetime, but never for a single hour or a single night. Hardly an evening passed in the weeks just after the unpleasantness with the bank that more than a few men didn't climb the steep hollow stairway out of the alley, out of the dark street or the black silent country or the hard saloon light to Marcel's room — and just to see Marcel: no choice, no lineup of shapes and sizes and colors of hair or gowns, no soft parlor, no piano music or drinks poured with a flourish by a Negro in white coat at the small intimate bar; and after each man left her Marcel would sit on her bed, her fading gown draped over her knees, and stare into the close wall as though she could see through it, down the street and around the corner and right into her old house and all the girls with their lavish luring of patrons, and she would smile at the new day's ending to her story.

As her lean roll of savings was again beginning to show signs of fattening, opportunity came, as it always had and, Marcel was certain, always would with another day. Two of her men friends, two of the oldest and best of them, had a business. It was a brisk busi-

118

ness and, since it involved breaking a law whose existence was widely ridiculed, respectable. They sold whiskey to the Indians on the reservation, thereby getting an impressive share of the money the government taxed out of the people for tribute to futility. The pair had engaged in the business for a long time and enjoyed what their notoriety and their talent with firearms rendered an exclusive franchise. They had a place in the business for Marcel and she accepted it.

Marcel would be in a position to handle certain situations that had proved awkward for the men; there were women among the Indians who disapproved of their husbands' use of liquor in the quantities the merchants supplied, and some cooperated with federal authorities who were trying to halt the liquor trade. In the beginning, Marcel's comings and goings aroused no suspicion around the reservation; also, it was presumed that any United States marshal in his zeal to stop the trade would not have been the kind of man who would demand to search a woman. There had, in fact, never been and probably never would be any marshal around with such scruples where Marcel Jones was concerned, but the security that Marcel's role suggested added a boldness to the trade. It grew more and more brisk and more lucrative.

Along with this new source of income, Marcel continued in her true life work; she made money faster than ever before and spent vindictively, doing huge business with the good, bosomed dressmaker below her room, holding her head high on the street that had used her so crudely, past the little stone bank that looked more like a jail than the jail itself, past the corner of the once-turning to the house, knowing that there were eyes at the windows and thinking of soon buying another house, one in which she would live by herself, bringing in the best of everything from the East, even perhaps a small silky combed dog such as ladies led across magazine pages, a stable, too, with a carriage and horse. Then her own good fortune that had come to her in one day turned on her in another day.

The Indians, after free use of the copious supply of liquor they were now getting, went off their reservation and conducted a few raids. The government used this opportunity to have the Indians moved out, onto land less desirable for white settlement and much too far away for the whiskey trade. And something happened to Marcel, as though something had been gathered from her and carried away with the Indians. She studied her face in the mirror, she looked herself over in each of the new gowns she had bought, then with no gown at all, but she could not determine what was gone. Yet she had the evidence that something surely was: the men had nearly quit coming — or they came too drunk or too broke and wanting to borrow and talk and cry after the town had taken them. The rest of the time — most of the time — Marcel was alone with her chair and window again, the shawl she had crocheted through the previous hours of waiting, and the old Bible which she took to cracking in half-hearted superstition and reading wherever it fell open, still trusting and believing in the new day that had always been with her. But now, sitting just at the edge of her vision, was a frightful ugly monster that the hoarding story days had finally formed, and she carefully kept herself from looking aside to face it — only straight to the window and the parted curtains when daylight filled the street.

Through these curtains she saw the first of the visitors bringing a name she had heard over the years, yet never quite a name, for a name to be meaningful must evoke a thought that could be linked to a bed or a glass

120

or a new gown or a plate of food; but more came, and the name continued to sound and a meaning began to form around the short, flat name "Og Jenks." Marcel sat rocking a little in her chair, letting the chair rock her and sway the shawl hanging down off her shoulders, looking out the window at the slow life of the street and her thoughts were stretching, spanning too much time for the short moments that passed. More visitors came, old friends and near-strangers. Still the monster sat off in the shadows at the edges of her eyes, and as she faced forward she could only see Og Jenks — or couldn't quite see, for the face was a mass of words heard and overheard; she had never, she was certain, actually seen the face. She tried to untangle the twisted sketches in her memory, tried to fit them to the talk of the visitors who seemed to be trying to make over the whole picture, the famous one of the ugly man with no face. But they never actually talked of a face: they talked of a mine in ore tonnage and dollars per ton and a home down in the canyon and money in the bank; then the worded face would vanish for a time. In the end she had to look; she had to look squarely at Og Jenks or turn aside and face the ultimate in ugliness and terror waiting in the faded light, and she was still looking forward when she walked into the hotel lobby escorted by two of her well-wishing visitors; there in front of her was the face, one-and-a-half-eyed and beyond ugliness; struggling with beauty, it might have seemed. But there was no struggle in that face. Only a yielding to all that had been, was, or would be.

A small crowd had gathered in the lobby and in Marcel's moments of looking it grew and pressed, impatient, insisting, smiling and persuading. Still another day was happening to Marcel, and this time she was being given; the giver, the collective will surrounded her, and hers only the will to be acted upon by the moment, to be given and to receive that which was being given to her, this name without a face here in front of her, this tightening around her and the name of Og Jenks. Then the crowd exploded, graciously full of laughter which gushed even from the slant mouth in a windy roar and probably even from herself, for it seemed that everything must have happened as the crowd willed it, still tightening until Marcel and Og were pressed in a sort of embrace.

The crowd itself was a strange conglomerate: a banker, a gambler, an attorney, a trail drover, merchants, miners, a chambermaid, and a minister's wife, the whole of it proud and pleased by its outrageous concoction. Marcel and Og were as much the handiwork of a mob as a corpse dangling in a noose, and only when the outrage began to compound itself, when a few of the more trifling began to talk of a church wedding with flowers and gown with Og Jenks in a cutaway, did the new couple protest — and they protested together against the grain of the mob. They wanted no part of ministers and music and Marcel being pushed down the board walk in a wheelbarrow according to the deep tradition of the eighteen-year-old town.

Then when the mayor stepped forward with his small prayer book it was Marcel who protested — alone at first. The day, present time as it stood was still her own and she was having no book opened in front of her, no ring proferred by the jeweler standing at the mayor's right hand — not just yet.

She had only to turn to the women — the seamstress, the banker's wife, the laundress, the church choir leader, and two or three of the girls from the house to whom she had no more than nodded in a sometime passing in all these dispossessed years. The women,

122

separately and in a single female mass, understood. No one of them would have let the moment go by, pass into the obscurity of a lifetime; and these women of the town and the sprawling countryside, poor in their sex, these lonely scattered few who with all their hunger for their kind had never dreamed of being seen in one another's company, escorted Marcel off shopping — off to shop her way into the new life that was always coming, now old to some and a reachless dream to others, but a hope to all, which they seized every opportunity to share, wherever it might be found or turn up. And most of the town's merchants that day of the wedding saw something of Og Jenks's rumored fortune.

I I

THE GREENHEWN PINE BOARDS of the cabin floor were warped and ill-fitted, caulked with mud of the mine and gray dust raised by boots walking under the prune-dried sun and tamped solidly here where feet paused. Some of the boards were high-edged to catch a woman's heel and throw her headlong as nearly happened to Marcel while, pacing, she pondered the board bed with its twist of greasy blankets and an old quilt with batting gutted at the edges. She suspected that the whole nest was lousy.

The bed was one of several articles for pondering and setting aside for the time being. The curtains had come first and were still outstanding. The curtains: tender pink gauze with big blue dots sewn in by hand — they had been one of the more gleeful purchases day before yesterday, her wedding day — far more spirited than the white lace ones that hung in her tiny white room back in town and behind which she had hidden her face from the street and the world; nicer in their given way than any that had hung in the many windows of the prosperous days. They must be put up first thing, ignoring the odors of unwashed pots and clothing, of soaked-in pine smoke and tobacco and mold and mildew — odors of the animal dens into

which the womanless of the men had always with-
drawn in safety after their time of need, into which
she would never once in those days have considered
following. (Indecent thought, to follow them into their
filth after accepting the necessary fragments of it!)
She put the curtains up with many an indulgent
standing-back, head cocked, to move forward then
and embrace them and put their newness to her nose,
to rub their teasing rough netting across her cheek.
Then she built up the fire in the stove, went out and
drew water from the spring, boiled it and washed the
dishes, watching righteously as the rancid grease film
formed on the steaming surface. She threw out the
dishwater on a barren spot far from the cabin. Then
she heated more water, swept the floor with her new
broom, dashed hot water over it and swamped out.
She went back again and sniffed at her new curtains
against the newly cleansed air of the room.

Pleasantly weary, she put herself to considering the
bed. It was as she had always suspected a man's very
own bed would be, and this was precisely why she had
always preferred to share her own bed with a man
rather than being taken to share his. And she was
yet to experience this ancient and proper sharing. The
night before on the road from town she had slept in
the wagon while Og slept in his bedroll on the ground.
There was not room for the two of them in the wagon,
and there was something altogether crude — childish,
anyway — about lying with a man on the ground.
They had in a cloudpuffed midmorning turned the
bend out of open desolation into the shutaway seclusion of the canyon and Og, dropping Marcel at the
brooding cabin, had hurried off to the mine. Now the
bed: she would sleep here tonight regardless, for the
day had brought her here and would end her here
barefooted before the nailed-together frame holding

the flattened wad of bedclothes. She made the bed as smoothly as though it were clean and toward dark when Og returned she fed him, then took him into her made bed skillfully, with the learned sympathy of one woman whose livelihood was another's duty, another's pleasure, overlooking the familiar fumbling efforts to be strong and the early silent failures, regarding his final triumph with acknowledgment and response. Men were never so satisfying as when they failed; for pity, she thought, must be the greatest passion of every woman.

Thus began and ended Marcel Jones's first day in the far canyon off the big silent valley.

On the second day and in the first light of it she saw above her the face, the one she had spent the night with, not one of many of a single night but a single face of the past night and many future ones — really a single eye, an orbal mirror floating in the gray dust settling in from the predawn horizon. Within it she saw her own face, tiny as the face in an opened locket worn by one who loves deeply, and the many days and the many nights strung out in receding reflections behind it — strangely younger than the face she had looked at for the last time in the mirror before she left her room. There, in spite of all her efforts, she had seen time and had tried to tell herself that what a bear had done with one wipe of a paw the slow washing of sand might match with its thousand creases of days. But there was no mirror on any of the walls of the cabin, and the compulsory morning look could not force time upon her. Certainly in the blooded crystal orb of eye there was no time. Some women, and all girls, burned to see reflections of themselves adored; but Marcel had no beliefs to restore, and adoration had never been what she required.

Time had set her here and stopped with no apparent

notion of starting again in this air where even the columns of dust across the bare valley stood still as trunks of trees. At least this day now rising out of the window had fixed itself forever, the measuring intervals silent as a stopped clock and shadows gone out of the sunlight as images from a whitewashed mirror; Marcel yawned and stretched, pressing sleep gently out of her and spreading the width of the grinding bed, for Og and the eye-mirror were gone now. She must have fallen back to sleep out of her first predawn awakening, and Og had gotten up without a word and made himself something or other for breakfast and had taken his deep roiled silence out of the door and down to the mine. Marcel lay a long time where she had been placed, feeling no will to move or force to move her, thinking of possible other stirrings such as a breeze to cross her not-really-heavy thighs, for her single motion of the day had stripped the covers from her — a breeze or something to act gently upon her and require nothing of her. From this point her thinking drifted ahead through this second day here, onward to supper and afterward the bizarre experience of accepting Og — this time, she would insist, leaving the lamp burning so she could watch her face in the hanging eye.

She floated across the surface of her second day in Og Jenks's cabin and its events followed behind thoughts projected from the bed where she had lain long in the morning; the pressing moments of the day moved her into its mouth, with the lamp lit as she had seen it, herself looking back from the eye inflating with the expanding circle of blood heat around it. She was amused and delighted beyond all her expectations. The lamp was blown out and moments later another day came as would another and many more, up the half-day, half-world stillness of the canyon, out of the wideawake valley and into the sleep gloom inside the squared logs, seeing sunlight briefly and as she chose in her hand-picked moments of duty, her trips to the spring for a bucket of water, the hot wind occasionally invading the cool of the canyon from the naked valley; the embracing walls had chosen her (once she had been the possession of a white room drawn away from the world of chatter, laughter and motion to which she had been sure she devoutly craved to return), with no choice and no passion she remained and kept most of her hours within the walls. Having fed Og in the evenings, which she was unaccustomed to doing for a man, her nights then were all of time that retained some semblance of the way to which she had applied herself through most of her years, for Og had the accumulated needs of half a lifetime. The days were the drifting, and on one of them her drifting again brought her cheek against the pink and blue curtains, grown lonely since the first day, and she held one wadded and brushed at it with her whole face.

Marcel had a passion for the clean and orderly. That which was outside her body and exposed to eyes must be clean and goodsmelling, free of the odors and doings of darkness. This impulse, as had many others during the first days in this place, had remained deep asleep somewhere; now as she stood with her cheek against the curtain she fought the lassitude of lying in shade on a hot afternoon, in a warm ring of fire overlooked by frosty windows. But she must get up eventually and she did. In her sparsely worded connection with Og she dropped her newest wants and saw him receive them silently. Then she waited. When Og returned from his next trip to town he lifted down from the wagon items she knew were his replies, and she took them one by one with a shaded smile; the whitewash, new blankets of tough, coarse-woven wool but soft as fur, a colorful coverlet for the bed, the blue-flowered china dishes (cups and saucers, sugar bowl, and cream pitcher which she had described as being on a certain shelf in the hardware store and which must indeed have still been waiting there), a blue and brown scrolled rug for the floor (not quite the sort of thing she had wanted and had once picked for her own house but chosen by Og and, considering, adequate), shiny serviceable pots and pans, a tablecloth of lace not unlike that of her curtains, and embroidered napkins.

These were indeed new days, as unlike the first ones as those were unlike the days of her room in town. On the day following Og's return from town, and after he left in the morning for the mine, Marcel whitewashed the walls, carried the old bedding to the tin-can dump in the creek above the house and remade the bed with new blankets and linens, spread the rug on the floor scrubbed to the last crack, arranged new china and pots and pans along scoured shelves that had once held cans of coaloil and harness grease. Then she set the table with the new china, on the new cloth and napkins.

Her churning moments of work had pressed the sun to its perch high above the roof gable, and the door opened and Og's laced, wide-soled boot was planted at the edge of the rug, the second one thumping into the middle of the rug, and bent and gaunt and smelling of mine mud he licked the stretched slant line of mouth and aimed his eye around the room. With a deep unmouthed grunt he sat down in front of one of the flowered plates and let a long corded arm fall half the length of the tablecloth. Marcel, still seeing only the new habitation she had just made for herself, filled his plate and his cup then saw him ram food manlike into the space between his columned neck and matted hairline. She stared and stared again; she had seen before, but only now was she certain she saw the efforts of the hungry mouth, bits and droplets of food escaping from the lower corner as from a cracked vessel. A soaked half-chewed bit fell and stuck against the tablecloth.

She had to stare until her memory completed the story out of someplace among the days of her growing up in the orphanage near Baltimore where there were no mothers but many blackhooded sisters who moved always just outside the scene, the setting, as it happened, of the story — the story of an ugly twist of a face trapping a beautiful and possibly even highborn young girl through days and nights of eating and sleeping in a silent stonewalled place to which dawn was always trying to come; behind the walls of the orphanage (and here, true memory or a tale dreamed with open eyes, no less true; which?) the face in the tale mingled beyond the cleaving power of thought and forever with the image of Satan as conjured by the sisters, who might also have dreamed the tale themselves — and retold it. Into this, the stone-gray voices whispering over beads, walked her lost mother one day, dressed not in a black hood but in a wicked ragged shawl. Marcel had been nearly grown then, swelling in front and shamefully straining the hip seams of her orphanage uniform; she was needed to help her mother make a living — needed, it turned out, to make a living for her mother who remained in bed from that day until she passed away two years later, whether from illness or weariness of exerting the effort that meant staying alive.

Then Marcel removed the memory from her mind, as taking dirty dishes from a table. She would wipe off the spot of Og's befouling from the tablecloth as soon as he left again for the afternoon. In fact, she would fold the tablecloth and put the dishes back on the shelves boiled clean, as she had intended in the first place. They weren't for everyday; they were for whatever special days might ever be.

Og left as abruptly as he had come and Marcel did as she had planned, scrubbing the tablecloth and folding it away, boiling the dishes and using up a declining afternoon hour arranging and rearranging them on shelves: cups to right, plates to left; plates in center, saucers standing up behind cups or lying flat and stacked. When she could no longer put it off she stood and pondered the room, the miner's shack turned whimsically to marriage by a bride who could not conceive of the state of being married, and what then was Marcel Jones to do with the ludicrous cloth of starched proper woman that had wrapped itself around her? She knew a house, but now house was no longer a word — house of an all-time man dreamed by a solitary woman; house, in fact, of a man who was hardly the everyman who lived in other dim places and came briefly in single column to house as she knew it, themselves bringing house into being and maintaining it but never the building stuff of it, seldom taking its shelter for more than a day and a night and, when leaving, taking their lives, their distinguishing properties as men with them.

Marcel had thought, those days of staring alone through a strip of the world out into the town's street, of curtains and tablecloths and china. She had thought of making without the means to make, but now she made; what (and she tried hard to remember) had she thought she would do with all of it spread before her, unmoving? Married was the means and the means demanded to be understood and recognized. Then suddenly Marcel remembered an old thought. She went to the small box of her most personal belongings, unlocked and keyless for many years, lifted its worn

leather lid and took out a pen and ink and some laven-
der stationery, mottled and fading now so that she
had to finger through many sheets to find one that
might be presentable for the women who lived in the
world of houses and understood their condition of
marriage. She would write the note as she had once
thought it, inviting all of them to come and by their
being here, perhaps explain to her the state that they
shared — "invitation," as it turned out, penned in the
best hand she could recall from the rigid days of the
orphanage schoolroom, to her "friends and neighbors,"
and that indeed was what these others were, these
women rumored to be living in their little homes
scattered sparsely over the valley; a notice that she
would be holding afternoon tea three days hence to
introduce herself to her new community.

She spent the next morning studying the three
dresses she had bought new on the day she had stood
before the mayor with Og waiting through his struggle
to make words. Which to wear on this day and which
to save for the tea? For she was going, as she told Og
when he came home at noon, down to the store to put
up her invitation.

She was dressed from hat to hell, and Og's eye, as
he stood stalled in the doorway, swelled away from its
inflamed socket as it took her in. Then when she told
him she would want to take the wagon for her trip and
expected to be gone through the afternoon his whole
body burned to a readiness as though she had drawn
a gun; his formless face took on a form, giving its own
stuff to her mind to form the ancient twisted image —
for whatever Marcel had known in her life had been
given to her in some dream or other that she had lived.

She stood pinned in the white glare of the image
merging its own stuff and the stuff her mind supplied,
freezing and melting in her new clothes; every rag that

hung from her skin out turned foolish and unneces-
sary. Was she then going somewhere? The face, if surely it was, hadn't really asked; and the clothes, those
silly duds . . . Yes, she was going for certain; *it* couldn't
stop her from going, if she could only remember
where. Marcel had been slapped by men, beaten even,
and kicked once or twice; but when it was done, when
the beater, the slapper, the kicker had his time he was
gone and so was the moment of it; never, not since
something like her sixteenth or seventeenth birthday
when her mother died, had her free comings and goings ever been successfully thwarted — but here, now
and by a face that could fix a moment in silence deeper
than dug earth, a moment filled with command, wordless as a single eye. But now with words the mouth, not
the eye alone, spoke: "If you ever leave out of here I'll
track you, and try and see if you can hide. Can't. Leave
and you ain't no woman; you're a hog then and I'll
cut you up like one just butchered."

The eye had done it, the mouth was undoing it. The
face could have kept the moment, stopped the sun if
the mouth hadn't moved. She was going and she remembered where — to the store, to put up her invitation and her clothes were the best, the next best, for
she was saving the best for the tea; and she was going,
on her way right now, through the door, slanting body,
ugly face or no, and out to the wagon and she could
surely remember how to hitch a team, and on out of
this ingrowing canyon to the open valley to the store
where people stood and talked and bought and then
this canyon would never be the same, never again . . .
proper house and home from then on. She was going
right now. . . . She began by laughing.

"You'll cut me up. I'm dead then. It don't matter to
me if I'm dead and it never did; matter'll be to you,
ugly man. Matter like you never thought could be.

See that bed there? I'm dead and it's empty, except for you. Think you can get another woman to climb in there with you, take care of what you need and never mind that face of yours? Not hardly. Don't often come a woman looked at so many faces her eyes just quit looking. You cut me up like you say and you got an empty bed then. Just try it now, after you had me in there these weeks, and see how it is. Just try thinking on it. Go on, try — yes, you. I can see you're thinking all right; don't ask me how I can see thinking on that face, but I can. You're thinking good and plenty; don't like what you're thinking, do you? Too late for thinking, isn't it?"

She could only guess what he was thinking, for his eye was now turned downward to the floor and she waited. When she saw that the time was right she shifted her body as though it were still slim and full of the girl she still was; she patted her small hat. "Now I guess I'll be driving down to the store." Og's eye kept to the floor, but he didn't move out of the doorway and Marcel could see by the set of his body that he wasn't completely done in — never would be, that man; his very being was a doing in and nothing from outside him could do much more. But she had won her moment and her day, and at last she could see him shaking his head, barely moving it and with great reluctance from side to side, and she could hear him mutter, "No, I'll drive you."

12

IT WAS AN HOUR'S WAGON RIDE down to the ford, and once there they had to wait nearly half an hour for the long, slouching Harris boy to notice them and rouse himself to pole the ferry raft across the river to pick up their wagon. Og sat and cursed everything with his eye, and Marcel tried to shake the dull dust piecemeal from her new dress and tiny hat. They rolled onto the raft and slid across the brown, corded water on young Harris's spindly muscles; on the other side, in front of the store, Marcel gathered herself and stepped down while Og sat reins in hand staring as far as the wide, hot horizon would let him.

The store had by this time begun to draw at the spread of circular valley as a great city draws at its hinterland. The town was remote, an adventure; but to the small but respectable ranchers and their families, to the miners and prospectors who still clung in scant handfuls to the lifeless mineral walls, to the eternal fugitives whom the law wanted and those who had exaggerated their imprint on the world and fancied that the law wanted them, the store was a center of life week by week, the center of their daily thinking and scheming. On their days, bonneted women gathered on the long porch or in the cool reaches of the interior among the merchandise to exchange news and opinions and to share what they believed were exciting events. They received their mail and read it there, sometimes aloud, and in the wing of the building which had extended itself just enough to accommodate a barroom, handfuls of men gathered of an afternoon or evening along the short bar or accepted the table invitation of an occasional traveling gambler, hungrily working the back country and making for some distant and lush abattoir in a boom town, who might stop off in the valley for a few days and leave, fattened or lean. Surely if one lived in the valley or just off it the store was the place to come to extend life in proportion beyond the fences of the in-pastures, to know a living sound other than the bawl of an ailing child or a mating bull. It was the place where bodies chilled in the harsh open wind could rub together and warm each other, the one place where a mind maddened with privacy could heal itself in public noise.

Whatever day or days of the week the store sucked in the life of the valley, this was not one of them; its emptiness today, haunted with the ring of frequently peopled places, rattled with two ranch wives far in the distant interior handling some yardage goods at a counter and mouthing words, an old man sitting habitually beside the summer-dead stove and a Negro leaning at a near counter, his face reflecting dimly in Marcel's teeming memory. None looked noticeably toward Marcel as she passed through the long line of food stocks with its blended odor, leather goods and hardware, hamed harness and readymade clothing, all at the high markup the valley paid or faced the day and a half to town through the heat and dust of summer, the sleet and wind and farther drifts of winter, the mud of spring and always the cost of an overnight stay in the hotel or setting up a family camp at the edge of habitation, dressing, undressing, washing, shaving, nursing babies and slapping children in near-public.

Marcel stopped to run her hands through some buttons, then some yarns. She felt eyes upon her.

She stepped on, face tilted and eyes forward, to the counter where Harris stood with some sort of smile. She handed him her invitation and he tacked it up, swinging the hammer with a flourish, on the spot near the honeycomb of postal boxes right behind the cash box and turned to her, still with a smile and, as she thought, something like a bow. Then she turned and walked out of the store, knees and hips stiffening, and mounted the wagon to ride back to the canyon with Og and wait the days she had imposed upon herself.

The next day she cleaned the house even more diligently than she had on all the other days, tired out before her time by unskilled and extravagant motions; for her knowledge of a house did not include the cleaning of one — that had always been taken care of by one or another of the hired girls or by the colored man who had once worked for them for a few months in the days when Marcel owned the house; but there was something absorbing, she found, even satisfying about the work for its own sake and she put her whole body into it, emptying her mind, pleased by the tingling ache of muscles and amused by the paper-dry ribbed skin of her fingers that recalled the wooden box they had stood her on at the orphanage when her age brought her to the task of dishwashing.

Then she rearranged the few sticks of furniture and stood in the center of the room, turning slowly.

If only she could somehow get to town . . . two — maybe three — of the girls would do it; they were loyal enough and had the souls for little and improper games of mischief. They would sneak out of the house maybe two of the fine horsehair chairs and let Marcel bring them down here in the desolation to her little married-woman's cabin just for the little while she would need them; then she would take them back and sneak them into the house the same way and they would all, remembering some of the little playspells they used to have, stifle giggles as they lifted them back through the window and got them into their proper places in the small morning hours, maybe with nobody ever noticing that they had been gone. Perhaps they would even help her get out the long settle she knew must still be in the parlor with the afghan draped over it waiting for evening and the merchandise to be lined up along it for the counting and choosing. She could see it now, right here in this unlikely cabin against the whitewashed wall, the rear one with no window, the ranch women, their one-man, child-bearing thighs planted on it, sipping Marcel's tea.

With fast-tiring limbs she rearranged the room again and quit. This must be her home, all right, since she had drifted here; and if out of the beyond and un-known outside the walls of her little canyon some im-pulse such as her invitation displayed far below inside the speck of building on the valley floor set others to drifting, carrying them to this spot, they would certainly see immediately that it was her room, the room that was all her home, just as it was and as she saw it now, taking it stick by stick into her being; they would see her in this subject-matter of her inevitable world, however differently the eyes of such women of God's flock might see. Besides, there was money (not under the bed; not on any shelf or in any rusting receptacle, relic or residue of the man called Hus-band's former miserable life here; no space between the logs of the walls big enough to accommodate the tin box copious enough to hold the reputed fortune — but perhaps under one of the floorboards, as had been rumored: she hadn't really put her mind and her energies to the search yet); there was enough to buy them all out and many more like them, you bet, and then buy back the house the bank had swindled her out of, although she wouldn't have it now as a gift and two more like it. Let the room stand as it was, shabby and respectably clean; who of them could afford to buy elegant furniture and freight it into the valley? and the affording of it was what mattered, not the buying of it. She tossed her head and walked to the mirror. The mirror — among the first items transported from town.

Yet when the morning came Marcel awoke with a dread. A little of the dread, but not much, went out the door with Og and his days of silent disapproval — frowning, if it were indeed possible for Og to frown. She was sure that he wouldn't be home at noon for dinner as usual, or in the afternoon or any time, until the last wagon or carriage or buggy or buckboard passed his mine going out of the canyon, assuring him that the world had put itself back in its place, far from him; then he could come out of his dug hole in the side of the hill. Marcel pulled herself out of bed and immediately began to clean and arrange again, first making the bed and smoothing the new cover over it, stamping at wrinkles in the rug and swatting flies, spreading the tablecloth and laying the napkins and china and standing back to look down at it, then above it at the oval gilt-framed portrait of the fine belaced elderly lady which she had crated from place to place these years and told, and now believed so thoroughly that she had forgotten just where she had really gotten the picture, that it was a portrait of her great-grand-mother rescued from the plantation house the day the Yankees burned it to the ground.

Midmorning she put her cake in the oven and tried

to forget about it after she had tried through its tedious mixing and blending to remember all she had ever heard and overheard with disinterest about baking a cake; and her one distraction was another fanciful glimpse of Og hiding like a hunted bear in his den, glaring one-eyed out on a hunting world and waiting for night. With the first sniff of the baking cake Marcel remembered that she had eaten nothing since getting out of bed and let the thought pass with a protesting pain from her stomach and an empty belch; and for the rest of the morning she tiptoed the floor as Frances used to order everybody to do when there was a cake in the oven, as there was every Sunday in Frances's time — every Sunday the cherished chore of the frail girl with gray skin and pink cheeks and bright fevered eyes, up to her last day which happened to be a Monday when she died coughing and gagging and reaching back toward the living as she bled speechless from the nose and mouth, finally leaving the rest of the girls in the house to finish her Sunday cake. A bit after noon Marcel opened the oven and let her breath out; the cake had not fallen.

Then, much too early and she knew it, Marcel filled the teakettle and put it on the stove. An hour later it had boiled nearly dry, and she looked down at her feet and saw that the last of the water was gone from the bucket; it was a bad moment, for it meant a trip to the spring and she, for reasons she didn't quite understand and hardly bothered trying, didn't want any of her guests to arrive as she was carrying a bucket to the house. She opened the door a little and peered out, listened to the silence out of the valley and the roar of a barely felt breeze in the wooded canyon; then she snatched up the bucket, ran to the spring, dipped it and hurried back to the door and closed it behind her before her good sense could tell her that it was too early by at least an hour to be expecting even the earliest of guests for tea. She refilled the teakettle. Then she made another trip across the room to look at herself in the tiny mirror with a corner of the frame chipped off, tilting it downward to see the hem of her dress then upward to catch her lined forehead and pile of graying hair. She could believe it, the proper woman with a proper and wealthy husband giving the best of herself to a proper home; why shouldn't they?

She reached down the cups and saucers and small plates, fitting their blue designs to the clothed table and wondering whether she had enough dishes, enough cake, enough tea. Her best count from hearsay had been fourteen women in the valley within driving distance of the canyon, counting unmarried girls old enough to be brought by their mothers to a tea. She had eight cups and saucers and nine plates — the odd one with the gold rim and faded gold lettering that told of some fair attended at a greener time in a greener country, a fat hog and blades of promising corn attesting to its hospitality to man, given to her one time by a manfriend of the evening who said he had no money and swore the plate was bone china trimmed in genuine gold leaf.

She plastered the frosting on the cake as it cooled, again remembering Frances, patching the holes as they appeared unexpectedly and licking her fingers and thinking how unsanitary that would appear to the wives if they were to see her doing it; then she sloshed out the teapot with boiling water and spooned in the tea leaves which came at a high price in that country and which, they would understand, she and her husband could well afford. Through the washed window the sun lay bright and silent over the rocks and brush and she worked against the shadows as they formed in the hollows, timing the passing of afternoon. Perhaps the slow gain of time meant that not so many would come and that was just as well. The cake would hardly go around. Perhaps she should have baked one yesterday and one today, for the narrow oven was only large enough for one.

The teapot went cold. She scooped out the soggy leaves and sloshed out the pot again with boiling water the way she had always seen her grandmother do it. She had never known a grandmother, but she would say that and believe it, for the one freedom she understood was that of believing whatever she chose and by believing making it true for herself and for anyone to whom she passed it on as she had in the past, filling up empty time and making memories which she otherwise would never have possessed. The teakettle was nearly boiled dry again. She dipped it full.

She turned back to the table and counted cups, felt of the hardened white icing on the cake unpleasantly streaked with knife marks, felt the warmth of the teapot and saw again in the mirror the matron maintaining herself, with a grandmother who knew of teapots and a great-grandmother framed in gilded oval on the wall; the odd plate screamed at her from the table and she stared at it, its unbelonging, tried to form a story of it but it would tell her nothing, nor could it distract her from the window toward which she edged and peered from behind the curtain and after a time standing full and bold and staring out at the dark shadow pools and the long ladder lines of the several pines in the hollow below the house edging across the uneven grass as the sun fell and failed. The dragging day drew at her in a way she understood; she resisted but the will was weak as sunset. Just then her ears plucked at a faint far rattle and clack.

She popped behind one of the curtains making the most of its frail shelter and straining through it to the outline of wagon road that led from her shut door out of her closed canyon and into the valley into which she had extended herself over all these later days. She was sure, then not so sure, that she had heard the turning wheel, turning in her direction. She waited a long time hearing the aimless workings of the creek below, feeling its way out.

Then the sound came no more, and when time finally quit moving she stepped to the door and threw it open. Deep afternoon struck her in the eyes and shading them she stepped down from the stepless doorway, turned her head and saw the swollen inflamed sun stuck on the tips of the rim trees and through the worn haze of spent day the flat brown of the road with its tufts of grass growing in a vanishing mound between wheel ruts where ground had grudgingly yielded to Og's wagon, and to no other. The breeze was gone from the canyon, an open mouth that had quit breathing, and the dust motes barely crawled in the unmoving air that mingled at last with that of the valley.

13

DEEP INTO THE TWILIGHT Og returned. He closed
the door behind him and stared long at the cold teapot
and the unused cups and saucers laid out on the tablecloth carefully cleansed of the blemish he had once put
on it. Then he stared some more — at the uncut cake
and the smoothed bed and the chairs arranged and
empty; but his stare communicated nothing, no more
than had the uncommon plate set apart from the
matching set, now no more and no less than the ones
that belonged. He could have been satisfied, relieved
that this retreat of his, opened thoughtlessly to the
world, had held so well. Whatever might have been,
his stare was the same one that always began and ended
each day and froze like marching icicles the hours in
between.

Og sat down to the table and Marcel heated the kettle of saltside and beans. Soon she would be watching
him ladle them onto a half-inch of stale sourdough
bread (she had learned from Og to make it, from the
distasteful beginning of dipping her fingers into the
smelly, fermenting starter) and begin scooping the
product into the slant scar on his face, as indeed he did
while she watched the odd and now commonplace
ritual, her eyes still strangely drawn to it but now fixed

in near-indifference as single beans in their juice fell like slow seepage to the once-prized tablecloth. And how was it that his sight still aroused in her a pang of disgust? How was it she had been unable to put it in the tight compartment she reserved for some of the other things associated with men — the services she in the line of her trade had learned to perform for them, the things she had learned to do with her own mouth? She poured him coffee in one of the new cups and set it on a saucer; she poured herself a cup and sat down and fell on her plate of bread and beans, her stomach opening eagerly to the first food of the day and forgetting as the empty pains relaxed the many hours of sunlight falling then failing on the wagon road. She filled her plate a second time.

Og was done with his supper long before Marcel and when she finally finished and looked up she saw that the eye had fixed her, as had become its habit. It held and, as was its nature, still told nothing — nothing in such an overwhelming extreme that she took to wondering what her own face might be revealing. She could not name her feelings from within.

Then Og got up from the table and blew out the lamp. Marcel responded; to her it was as the grunting command given to a plow horse, grown so familiar over the years that she responded neither with pleasure nor resentment: it set her hands in motion where she stood, undoing the buttons of the tea gown and slipping it down over her shoes, picking and plucking at the laces of her corset, an article she had worn only for that single day and, as she thought idly, might never wear again, unbuttoning her shoes, unfastening her stockings and rolling them down. As she felt for the pinnings of her elegantly piled hair she heard mingled with its rustlings the whisper and snap of the ugly man's suspenders; in the dark these sounds were to

145

her every man's language, but, in the case of Og, these too told her nothing. Driven by old and weary impulses she hurried and got into bed. Og was still unlacing his boots.

Finally he came to her, but he didn't take her in a few fast strokes that were a man's way with a woman he had bought. He took her, but little by little, limb by limb as she lay accepting, feeling no obligation, as during her days in the trade, to give back, to make a pretense of repaying in kind. He was silent in his taking; even his breathing which usually sounded somewhat monstrous in his bent nasal passage was hushed, and his creeping, pressing slowed time to a single moment heavy with its flow as though he must eat and drink her totally and sweat her out of his skin. When he finally entered her it was like a long meditation ending in a quiet thought, the thought (and the only thought from him) which she received, the irrevocable fact of her drifting to this bed. She was no more a member of the world than was this man. This was the thought that contained the accident of her ending, here on her back and connected to this body that seemed a piece with the dark: he who had lived rejection of all that touched and was touched, repelling, drawing the excluding circle around his being until its circumference fit the single eye of his face; she who had sold and whose merchandise had given the illusion of making her a place among the others, the objects touching and touchable that she was certain were truth. This side canyon had been her place even in the days out there of giving and taking and laughing and cursing; the nights of lamplight and piano and glasses, dark and heavy with breathing and coin on the bedside table; the days of long, late sleeping and the silk sheets in the heat of noon. She who had once had a bountiful stock of the wares they demanded was now

146

sold out, with no profit to show for it. The canyon was her place by default, his by choice. That was his thought that came to her in the end of it; that was the silent answer of those invited guests who had not come to verify the new life she had made, as she made everything meaningful, out of the stuff of her head. She lay awake a long time after he fell asleep with his back to her.

She was still lying on her back when she faced the gray morning and the lingering night in the pits between the hewn rafters. She heard the stir beside her where Og had fallen into his sleep the night before; he lifted and hovered above her, the eye hanging there a moment like a smooth dull stone. She came out of the bed behind him and for the first time made him breakfast. He ate without a word, without another look toward her, and left for his mine leaving her still another aimless morning of drifting between disjointed acts. At midday Og entered the door heavily and sat for his meal and left her with a stunned afternoon which somehow fell away to dusk when Og came home again, fed his mouth and blew out the lamp; he crept into the bed beside her, again like a piece of the dark, again spreading himself slowly over her, telling her bit by bit, touch by touch, movement by movement who she was and where she belonged.

Again the days were pulsing past, each like another; the clouds refused to rain and the air refused to move in wind and even the birds seemed unnerved by the expanded silence, talking in hushed chirps; the creek weakened with the dry season, the sound of it diminishing to a moist rattle while the sun dulled the brittle green of the trees and curled and yellowed the grasses. Twice each day, seldom oftener, Marcel went to the spring for water and sometimes paused to stare down the road she had once come up, the road nobody ever

147

took and which led only to some other canyon, some other room wrapped in curtains. At nightfall a single sickly breeze blew like a gale and died into the dark, with lamp out and light gone and Og covering her, coating her through successive nights like a slow-lived growth, and the word "love," as she had heard it spoken, occurred to Marcel — it could be just that, for all Marcel knew, and if it were love, Og emitted it as other men emitted their juices — their waste that pressed them with discomfort until such as Marcel drew it out of them and accepted their money for the service.

Yet, one day set itself apart from the others. Marcel had awakened with a lightness in her head and a long-forgotten energy in her body. After Og was gone she left the cabin with her bucket and walked carelessly toward the spring, her head bouncing high and away with every step, sure she could if she chose strike the sky with her palms or kick her foot to an unknown depth into the earth; and when she came to the spring she let the bucket fall with a rolling clatter and stood looking around her, certain she had never really done this before but had always let the bucket fall into the water to fill and drew it back and hurried to the cabin. But now she glanced only briefly down into the clear water hardly disturbing the daylight it contained in abundance by its lively pouring out from the rocks, barely moving the clean gritted bottom; the living sight of its small act of unceasing creation caused her to look up and out at the rocky ridges, the brush thickets and gloomy patches of pine in the faded green of willow and sycamore. Her legs were moving her then, taking her first to the road which straightened out before her as she walked along it and led far beyond the bend and downward and outward onto the sea of bright dry air and sky. The world was growing,

148

outside the canyon which now seemed to let itself out onto a shoreline with an ocean beyond moving and restless and angry, containing and multiplying all the forces that had pushed and tossed and drifted and held her fixed. She saw the slow-flying magpies drag long tails up into the trees, saw a ground squirrel skitter, another behind it, and a large beetle fighting the dust to escape her feet as she passed. The squawk of a jay seemed to call out a small rattling breeze that sank back into sleep, and so did the other days; for she was moving, not on the swaying steps of days, but on her own feet, and she doubted that they would ever stop now and she could not remember back to the standing and waiting, even to the standing at the spring and the first breaking look outward, expanding inside her with the scope of her eyes. She began to hum a tune.

And the tune carried itself a measure beyond her steps. Her feet had stopped in their tracks, but she still heard her voice humming. Directly in front of her face hung the eye. Yes, surely it was Og, standing in the road right in front of her, where the road had been empty and waiting for her step. He stood in a length that seemed to slant a little to one side, his torn mouth tight and his one eye large — large enough to hold her and the rocks and the trees and the sea of air and sky and valley. Her feet had stopped while it seemed that they were still walking, walking on and through him, where he hadn't stood but was now standing. The strange slant figure could have been doubted, but not the eye.

There was no answering where he had come from, nor did it seem a reasonable question; his being there was question and answer. She tried to remember that her feet moving and free of the ground had brought her this long way on the road from the cabin and could only feel what would seem to be the same feet now stuck deep into the bedrock below the soil, and the eye swelling like a bubble and appearing to lean toward her while the head and the standing form did not move. If only the eye would move, or the mouth make a word. He had stood in front of her this way once before, that day in the doorway long ago when she had told him she was going to the store to put up her invitation; and that time as now the eye had grown toward her, outward as though it would encircle her and lose her for all time in its nowhere — then in an instant to turn and become a receding, deepening cavern, drawing in, and eternity of the same nothing. Except that on the other occasion he had finally spoken, words of awake and chattering places freeing her tongue to talk back to a mere man with wants and discomforts, needs and pleasures, weakness and doubt and she had in the end been the one with the strength to carry him away — to where she wanted to go. But he was not going to make the mistake this time; he was not going to speak. He was not going to talk of death and threats and knives and hogs and absurd things that swept away fear; he was just going to place the eye there in the road in front of her — the eye that was not the property of fear but was fear itself, that gave her no object to recognize as the maker of fear.

After a long time the eye seemed to draw back into its socket and become as much an eye in a face as it ever could be, and Marcel found that she could lift a foot from the ground, found that she could turn around and did, and walked back toward the cabin, strength drained from her, her head heavy now and unspirited and with a will only to get back and close the door against the harsh sunlight. She did not turn around to see whether he were following because she knew he wasn't, and she knew that if she were to turn she would find the road now as empty as it had been when she had walked down it.

Back inside the cabin the stale gloom folded around her and she welcomed it. She sat down on the bed and looked around at the small life, the last of many she had made for herself, and was sure that she would never leave this one and probably never again give a thought to venturing far into the sunlight. The old lady who was a stranger looked down on her out of the oval frame, the eyes pale, trying to be haughty in her lifelessness; Marcel's gaze followed around the corner of the room to the plates standing up on the shelf, the blue design on one of them printed just a trifle off center; she noticed too that one of the cups had lost a handle and wondered with little concern where and how it had happened; directly beneath the shelf squatted the little oval stove, tiny but adequate to heat a single room and to cook a meal for two; and all around and in and among these things, this room, mostly something of Og Jenks. Whenever he left in the morning something of him remained in the room, about the house no matter how intensely or how often she might rearrange it, speaking as loudly as did his silence when he came home at night, as did the eye hovering over her in the lamplight on that far evening or hanging in the middle of the road in the high morning. It was not in this remote canyon nor in this cabin nor in this room that Marcel's life had lodged. It was in the eye.

14

A CLEANSHAVEN YOUNG MAN with small, lively blue eyes and a white brutal face tied his horse carelessly in the punishing sun only a few yards from the cooling shadow of the eaves, slipped easily to the ground and swung up to the porch and through the door. The big room of Harris's store was gloomy as twilight, and as empty and silent. With long, light, loose steps he strode across the room, his eyes shifting from right to left, to the farther reaches where Harris rose up out of a wooden armchair and stepped behind the counter. The young customer looked the storekeeper over critically and took his time about speaking up.

"Need some things," and he chewed at the words as at chance particles washed from between his teeth. The tone was flat and coppery as he began listing his needs, turning from time to time for an incidental glance at the door.

He recited the items of purchase rapidly, a sharp note of impatience in his voice whenever the slightly deaf Harris asked him to repeat, as though he had never in his life had need to stop and think, decide, remember. The items were all of saddlebag size, such as canned and otherwise preserved foods for a frugal and hasty diet, tobacco and coffee. At the end, he asked for a small ration of corn in a gunnysack and a box of forty-four-forties. When he had gathered his purchases into a bundle and paid, he turned abruptly and left the store with the same hurried but casual steps.

He hastily arranged his supplies in the saddlebags and untied, mounted and kicked his horse into a running walk out onto the wagon-widened trail that meandered across the valley floor. As he rode, his eyes wandered up, down and all around the far walls that shut in the valley as one trying to put to immediate use some half-remembered knowledge of the place, draw upon a store of hearsay and place it in present time — seeking to match old landmarks to memory and fix new ones among the slow-turning bluffs with their clinging trees and sparsely-forested crests, his far stare leaping the featureless valley floor that was distinguished only by the winding strip of trees that marked the course of the river. Occasionally he shot a quick glance behind.

A trace of bewilderment crossed the otherwise expressionless face as he scanned the vast, walled hole that cupped him: the valley was both known and unknown to him, as it was to all who lived and moved in a region one third of a continent, especially those who had broken laws and perhaps also those who saw deep within themselves the possibility of breaking a law sometime or of flouting the unyielding rules of community; they all knew of the valley, whether they had been there or not — knew of it because of its unknowableness, a far, secluded place still safe for the habitation of misthoughts and misdeeds. Of the people who lived here, even those who were not breakers of law or convention, good citizens who had begun to people the valley, chose not to talk or show friendly faces to the chance lawman who might wander in; the lawmen seldom came, for they had heard talk about others of their calling who had entered the valley and were never again seen outside. And although the valley had begun to be settled, these small incursions affected neither its intrinsic character nor the stories told about it.

The stories were many; in time they blended together in everlasting confusion, their characters having no real distinction: there was the army deserter who hid . . . but was that the freighter who had vanished with the wagonload of gold bars? . . . or the Mormon bishop who deserted wives, community and children to run off with a common whore and set up a saloon for train-robbers and cattle thieves. . . .

The rider's large, soft-lined face tilted again and turned as his eyes made another sweep around the circling rim, pausing now and then at a darkened fold which might have been an accident of the slanting sun or, again, might have marked the entrance to a secluded and secure canyon with a plentiful running stream and waist-high wild timothy headed out in rich seed to feed a horse and save the few handfuls of corn in saddlebags; where there were grouse, rabbits, sage chickens and deer to feed a man handy with his gun and keep a small store of food from dwindling too fast. A time or two he started to neckrein his horse off the road, frowned indecision into the distance, then changed his mind. A few houses were visible far off — a few, but just that many more than hearsay pictured; twin wagon ruts, a horse trail — either one might end in a dooryard, presenting the new and unknown. The worn road seemed a surer thing, a trail of earlier times and older tales.

Memory jogged loose another of the old stories — of the man so ugly that few people could look him square in the face, so good with a knife that he never had need to take a gun in his hand, so mean that he

154

would and could kill anybody or anything half his size or ten times his size that just happened to walk close to him when he was in the mood for killing, so rich that he probably did not know himself how much was in the tin box he kept hidden around his cabin someplace. He couldn't abide anybody and nobody could abide him, so he lived alone — no, not anymore, so another story had seemed to go . . . married; the woman that used to run the hookshop in town living up there with him now, and the mine that had made him so rich, up in one of those side canyons and nobody seemed to know just where, talked as though it were hidden, lost, or maybe there was no such place, maybe the story that sounded too much like just that — a story. . . . The young stranger's eyes kept scanning the valley rim with something like a purpose and darted hastily behind him now and then. He seldom looked forward, where the road was taking him.

Down the road, far ahead in the distance, two specks moved as a double figure. They grew and took shape until they could no longer escape his notice, and when he finally did see them his eyes held them, his body stiff and alert, his face quivering. He reined his horse in to a slow walk and took another quick look around him; then he spurred boldly forward as though eager to meet what was moving toward him, his big right hand sliding from the pommel and slowly forming a cup as though to shelter the stock of the revolver in the scabbard at his belt.

It was in this posture that he closed the gap between himself and the Negro on muleback leading another mule fully packed and bristling with mining tools.

Dot looked at the hand hovering over the gunstock and grinned.

"Now you, so young and full of livin' — aimin' to help a old nigger man get out this miserable world?"

155

Dot was only as old as he chose to be, and now old only in contrast to the empty youth of the rider's face, the small blue eyes that studied Dot with a slow sort of pleasure having adhesion to the inflicting of pain, torment, or death; but at the moment, interfering with this larger purpose was a flutter of animal fear. The young man measured the older one with the black face slouched on the stunted mule as though trying to decide what action might most please or profit him.

"It ain't goin' help you none to kill me. . . . Now mind you, I ain't sayin' harm'd come to you if'n you was to shoot me right here, cause ain't nobody care enough about me to come ahuntin' you down. It's when you kills one of them that the law-abidin' folks thinks high on that you makes a mistake. But it just ain't goin' gain you no profit to kill me, mainly cause all's I was fixin' to do was maybe pass some friendly talk then go on my way, mindin' my own business."

Some of the fear faded from the face, but a slow-witted suspicion replaced it. The hand remained near the revolver stock.

"What I'm noticin' about you, young Murphy, is you looks mighty tired."

Young Murphy did not look tired; in fact, there was a physical alertness about him. But Dot's abrupt observation had its effect. The puzzled listener showed signs of beginning to reflect on his own condition, turning his attention away from his concern for the sudden encounter.

"Now there's the big difference between a old critter and a young'n. Us old ones, when we gets tired we knows it all over, and right then and there we lays us down and takes a good snooze, and if'n that don't help none then maybe we just goes ahead and dies and gets it done with; but you tadpoles, well you just keeps goin' — ain't the good sense in your innards to tell

156

you you's all in; and then you just drops right there with your feets still agoin', maybe drops dead, without ever the time for knowin' there was somethin' goin' wrong all the time. Reckon you been ridin' a long far spell, from the sweat patches and lather on your horse. Ought to stop and let him blow a bit in the shade — and you too. . . . Now that there's all I got to tell you, young Murphy, and you look like you ready to shoot me dead for it. Don't make no sense."

Young Murphy, obviously bored and impatient with Dot's slow talk, seemed somehow compelled to listen a little longer, his reservations showing in the squinting stare of his small eyes, the tightness of his mouth, the twitching fingers of the hand that still hovered near the black-checked hard-rubber revolver stock. His horse, fully as weary as Dot had described him, rocked slowly where he stood, planted a foot forward and attempted to drop his head to rub his nose against his foreleg. Murphy gritted his teeth, snarled, and jerked the head up with a sharp tug at the bit. The horse stood patiently and the rider showed no signs of moving on. The two of them effectively blocked the narrow road to Dot's two mules. Dot, with the skill of one who had faced and survived many such encounters, talked on:

"It ain't proper between strangers for one to ask where another's goin'. And you and me ain't never met and talked in such a way as to say we ain't strangers, so I don't never ask such. But I see you ridin' along, lookin' all around, makin' like to turn off'n the road now and again — like maybe you's havin' a hard time to make up your mind where you's at and where you wants to be."

Murphy's head weaved with annoyance as he crouched toward Dot; his mouth worked, clamped shut, finally opened a crack to let out a few rattling,

rapid words. "Seems anybody can see I'm travelin'
down this road, so it looks like I'm goin' where this
road leads. Maybe you got some more questions." The
tones were low, both throaty and nasal, speech alien
to this region — the unfamiliar speech of one of the
far sections of the country that had mixed thinly into
the process of settlement.

Dot's face spread into an unhurried grin. He turned
slowly and pointed down the shimmering road to the
hazy cliffs at the far end of the valley.

"This here road? That the one you figures to travel?"

"Ain't that what I just said?"

"Then I reckon you don't know much about where
you goin', and maybe you best listen to what I got to
say about roads. This here one, it run straight and flat
and easy down yonder the way you sees it; then you
don't see it no more and that's because she ain't no
proper kind of a road once she start climbin' and
windin' up amongst the rocks and brush. What you
sees now is the road that the ranchin' folks hereabouts
uses to get here and yon, to the store and maybe to
town, but once she get to them bluffs yonder they ain't
no ranchin' folks or much else — no road, that's sure.
She just a trail that switch back and switch back, up
and sort of gentle in a way of speakin' till you comes
to a bad wash bustin' straight down the cliff. There's
where you gets off your horse — and you stops to let
him blow a bit if'n you wants to keep him under you
for the time comin' a good bit later when you can
climb aboard him again; what I mean, it's too much
climb and too rough goin' for ridin' and you leads
your horse straight up and the thorn brush rips your
face up a bit and tears your clothes to the bare skin if
you ain't got leather up to your neck, which you ain't;
and after while daylight givin' out on you, and then
the goin' start to get bad. Maybe you don't get to stop

158

and set till sunup. Then again maybe you makes it up over the rimrock dark or not. Say you does. Ain't nothin' up there but flat high desert and not a trickle of water for a day ridin'; only the way we just done told it it's still night yet and you just falls out the saddle — flat ground look that good to you. You got a powerful thirst from the climb and you aches and hurts all over, and your horse is give out by now, if he ain't long before. You done use up all your water and they's none for your horse neither, and you got a dry day ahead. If your horse hold out and you don't take a wrong way you gets to Shortleg Crick along sundown, and she's down mostly to mud this time of year. You got somethin' to dig with, you digs up some water. Me, I ain't lookin' to know what's outside up there cause I already done seed it."

A weariness slowly settled over Young Murphy as Dot talked. His right hand had forgotten the revolver and now rested again on the pommel, the shoulders drooped and the eyes widened into a despondent stare at the cliffs far ahead. He seemed willing to listen further to what Dot had to say — too willing, for he was still not ready to move aside and let Dot go on his way. He looked over, for the first time it seemed, the bags and tools hanging from Dot's pack mule.

"You been minin'?"

"Minin'?" Dot shook his head. "Don't hardly name it such. I been apokin' and adiggin' here and yon, but don't hardly find nothin' like a mine just yet. They's such around here though — as to make a man want to keep on tryin'." Memory led Dot's eyes along the valley rim behind and to the left of where Murphy sat in the saddle; he nodded absently toward the point of his far gaze. "I used to be partners in a copper mine once — mine worth more'n ten men could spend in ten lifetimes. But not no more. I ain't partners no

159

more, but that's the way of things. Sometime I find me a mine of my own, and ain't no partners then."

Murphy turned in his saddle to follow Dot's gaze. He picked out a triangular shadow that broke the tall valley cliff top to bottom: the mouth of a canyon or an accident of the lengthening sun? Both were silent a long time, the talk of chance meeting between two unlikely travelers on a barely formed road nearly ended. At last Murphy straightened and gathered his reins in his hand.

"Think I'll go back, you goin' on that way?"

The voice turned Dot abruptly from his far stare at the valley wall.

"I reckon I'll go on down and set at the store a spell. Seems like that porch and chair in the shade lookin' good to me these summer days. Maybe be my undoin', I don't get out and rustle a bit, but the settin' spells gets longer every year."

Dot looked at the sun-pinkened face — the fear that Murphy might have concealed effectively from nearly anybody but Dot had largely gone from it, and Dot, too, relaxed inside and kneed his saddle mule and led his pack animal around the horse, which turned without a signal from its rider and, as a horse will do in the presence of mules, followed senselessly the two odd creatures and caught up with them.

"Any place down below shallow enough to get a horse across the river?" Murphy asked.

"Well, they's the ferry, a'course. But back about half a mile yonder side of the store takes off a road to the right, and right there's where I always cross the river." The store had just come into sight, a low speck of a building far down the road, and Dot pointed just to the right of it along the bright green strip that marked the course of the river. "It ain't really no road. I don't say you can't miss it because you can, sure enough. It's just a couple old wagon ruts and they's sagebrush to hide a horse down there in the bottom where the river flood over in the spring, scruboak and chokecherry just before you comes into the river trees. You gotta pay close mind or you sure miss it. Right there you takes off into the river. She easy enough to get a saddle horse across — a wagon and team, too — cause ain't nothin' but solid sand and gravel bottom, no quicksand or muck. But don't nobody do it these days so everybody sposes it can't be did and pays to take the ferry. That's the way with folks."

They rode the rest of the way back to the store in silence, the young white man, the aging black man, and before Dot dismounted to tie up at the hitching rail, he pointed on downstream to a stand of young willows, the spot he had told Murphy a horse could be forded. He wished his young companion luck with the politeness of one relieved to see the other go on his way, tied up in front of the long porch, eyeing the inviting wooden chair deep in the cool shadow.

Murphy pressed on down along the river where the heavy-trunked cottonwoods grew in untidy line along a grassy island between a dry bed and the summer-shrunken water. He searched the banks of the river, first the near one then the far one, occasionally slowing his horse for a more careful look at some special spot that caught his eye. Dot had given him directions, but he appeared not to be one to follow faithfully the directions of another — a near stranger and a black man at that; directions could be taken for what they were worth when matched to what he saw for himself, in the manner of men who survived by putting their trust only in their own eyes and took the good wishes and advice of others merely as words for their ears. The washed banks of the river were covered by a heavy layer of coarse gravel, but here and there, where the water had receded from a summer of plentiful rains, flats and patted ridges of wet sand and solid mud glistened. Muck or quicksand? Could sink a horse that just set a foot into it by chance. Then his sharp little eyes picked out something that did indeed look like a faint trace of road leading down the gentle bank and entering the slow water at right angles. At first glance it looked more like deer or cattle paths, but the two parallel lines of wagon wheels stood out plainly enough after some study. They emerged from the water on the opposite bank still more plainly worn and wagon-rutted.

The horse, a strong, durable, spiritless gelding, showed only slight reluctance as Murphy gouged its flanks with his large-roweled spurs and pressed into the water. The sluggish current drew fine curved lines around the fetlock joints, and Murphy spurred again. The horse plunged on, the middle of the river was only flank deep. It was true then, what the old black man had said; the river could be crossed here. With new spirit, something close to enthusiasm, Murphy rode on across the river and the horse stepped with confidence on the gravel bottom and worked up the steeper bank on the other side and through the fringe of brush and trees. It was plain now that what had seemed to be a road crossing the river continued, wandering on across the slightly uptilted flat of shortening brush toward the steep side of the valley where the first cedars clung. Murphy followed it, and soon the opaque shadow between the two pointed columns of rock deepened into the entrance to a canyon.

The road steepened abruptly when it entered the canyon, upward and around a bend and the valley was lost, here where the world narrowed securely. The horse heaved a few more steps up the slope, loud hot breath reaching into the cool relief of the canyon, to where the cedars and piñon thickened and scented the air. The walls were steepening, rising high and leaning in. The sun was nearly finished crossing the short sky to the wooded ridge above. Murphy rode on, indifferent to the pumping muscles and heaving breath of the horse under him. The road — plainly now, that was what it was, cut in and clinging to the canyon wall and rising faster than the creek that fell farther and farther below in the bottom and was often lost in the foliage that crowded its banks.

A path darted off to the left and disappeared in the taller trees that now covered the slope. Murphy reined in. A path? More like a sideroad used by wagons and joining the one on which he rode. He kicked a foot loose, draped a knee over the pommel, and sat a long time, watching the sideroad as though some slow plan were forming behind his well-made face. He turned his head slowly from side to side and listened. A squirrel chattered, a crow called, the stream gurgled behind and below. The silence of the canyon was profound, close and narrow, unlike the wide silence of the valley.

The deep thump of an explosion shook the ground. Murphy's horse almost turned from under him. His face reddened, he snapped the severe bit sharply; the horse pranced and winced and stood subdued. Again he sat for a long time, listening and staring down the intruding sideroad, but the explosion had deadened all sounds to a ringing silence. He listened one last time, then cautiously reined around and rode on, past the black gaping mouth of the mine, the slagpile crunching underhoof — no story now; real as the sight of it gouged into the side of the hill, as the shaking blast of dynamite and the sounds of work deep inside. He hurried on at a trot and put the mine quickly out of sight again, nor did he show surprise when a cabin,

163

chimney smoking, low barn and corrals beyond it, leaped out from behind the last bend in the road. He rode on to the end of the road. He dismounted, dropped rein, and knocked at the door.

15

IN THE DEEP STUFFY SILENCE of one of her days came a startling knock; then another piece of the day slipped past in seasoned silence and the knock came again. This time she believed it, lifted herself from the bed and opened the door — opened it upon the teeming irrevocable manfaces of time gone: faces bearded and beardless, small and large, weak and strong, boy and man and aged, shallow and deep, but each one whole, with two eyes side by side and matching in size, straight-set mouths that could laugh and grin and sneer and frown; all fitted to the name Marcel Jones and in two instants of a knock and a cracked open door.

She opened the door wider and knew that she had smiled, although his latent face was looking beyond her and into the room. She made a single-word query and he didn't answer but passed on into the house and stood in the middle of the room, his eyes roaming at random; she asked his name and he replied with his own word, still not giving her a glance.

Yet in another sense it seemed to Marcel that all the questions had been asked, all the answers given in a year, say, of being what they called fifteen . . . in another year of being another age and feeling no different for it, no different from now. He was through the door, in the house from some elsewhere in the extended world with no canyon walls nor breathing mouths of rock; he did not seem to care to talk just now nor to look her over, which would have seemed reasonable; yet in this situation she could look him over at her leisure, which she did — young and sturdily put together, of course, with fair skin that knew wind and sun yet seemed to possess the exemption of young things, sweat-stained hat just that moment shoved back with a coiled lock the color of light mud toppling across a fleetingly furrowed forehead; feet in a firm plant, too firm to be sure of their footing.

Then he turned and walked out the still-open door; hungrily the room began closing around her again, until she saw him through the door, unsaddling his horse, then leading with one hand and swinging the dragging saddle in the other around the cabin and out of sight. He had gone . . . probably to the corral. In a short time he was back and this time he let himself fall heavily into one of the chairs close to the table, sighing and clamping his hand around his forehead. Marcel began to think of his needs: hunger, for instance, and she went to the stove and took the lid off the kettle: rabbit stew, with sodden half-sunken dumplings caught in the hardened broth, and she stirred the fire and moved the kettle to the middle of the stove.

She put a plate in front of Young Murphy and he ate desperately. When he was finished he told her in a few swaggering words that he was going to board here for a while and that he would pay when he got to it. Marcel motioned toward the bed and he stumbled across the room and spread himself across it, face down and spurs up, and dropped into a deep sleep. Marcel spent an uncommon late afternoon in the cabin sitting with her back against a far wooden wall under the stiff face of the elderly lady in the frame, listening to the strong breathing breaking into the many days of silence.

She was sitting that way in the early dusk when Og came through the door and stood long and stared at the bed and at Murphy who had hardly crooked a finger in his sleep. Og waited for the word that Marcel had to give him; but the tones when they came out of her were not those she had been hearing in her head all afternoon through Murphy's sleep breathing, nor were the words those she had intended. She had planned to announce flatly and firmly to Og that she had decided to take in a boarder because she needed the money for herself, since he gave her none to spend of her own choice (and she did not confuse the argument in her own mind by the consideration that she no longer had needs nor any place accessible where she could spend money). Instead she told him in a voice without force that she wanted to take in a boarder to have some extra money to put into the mine and added after a while that she wanted to do her bit to make the mine produce the way Og wanted it to so that he wouldn't have to work so hard.

Og sat down at the table, using his silence as he had become accustomed to do and leaving Marcel, in the end, without words. But her explanation seemed to have satisfied him for the time being, although she could read the disturbance in his posture, in the minute jerk of his head each time he pushed food into his mouth and in his hot puffing at his pipe after supper. When Murphy finally awoke he seemed to see neither of them. He stretched, slipped off his spurs and shoved them into his hip pocket, and walked out the door into the cool sounds of crickets and katydids.

The door closed across the sounds and the night

leaped into the distant outdoors beyond the yellow flickering walls where Marcel tried to listen while Og, his eye rolled down toward his bulge of cheek, squirted smoke from the higher corner of his mouth. When his pipe drew no longer and the last of the smoke had accumulated in the thin blanket under the low ceiling, Og got up, cupped a hand around the lamp chimney and brought the night inside, and Marcel began to work at her clothing with her ears still drawing at the sounds outside, hearing only the thoughtless throb of the crawling and hopping and not the broken uneasy sounds of a man. As usual she was the first in bed. Og crept in and began. Marcel, as she had mostly done in her life and, she believed, even the first time, turned her body over to duty, to perform the task without thought and let her mind go where it would — this time to the listening; and at last, through the man's struggles, she heard the door open, saw or felt the form standing briefly and heard the sounds of a bedroll being unrolled over near the stove in the area which, had there been a dividing wall, would have been the kitchen. Then, receiving the last of Og and disconnected from him, she went to sleep hearing the snapping dying of the stove and the doubled sounds of breathing.

Og left for the mine before dawn. Marcel awoke with the closing door and after the moments it took her to possess herself she remembered . . . a different sort of morning; that of a bare childhood into which something out of the ordinary had come the day before, long dream memories strangely merged with her own with a shadow or two for parenthood shading the imprint of old and unyielding cobblestones on small bare feet in another stone-gray city without a sun, the same robed figures dangling tiny metallic agony on beaded chains (and how was it that she knew and recognized so clearly that which her eyes had never before seen? How was it that a half-dozen surly words the day before now evoked so vividly her own small self of the infinite past out of another place and time?). She waited to give the new situation full attention until after she had heard the last of Og's footsteps. Then she got up in the dark and felt her way to the stove, stepping carefully around the spread bedroll, stirred and stoked and emptied the coffee pot of yesterday's brew that Og usually drank, half-warmed, tar-black, and corrosive, before he left but had passed up this morning, and filled it fresh. She placed it beside a skillet loaded with salt-side and heard a chill stirring of dawn wind outside in the trees and saw gray flakes of daylight at the window. She called to Murphy drawn deep down in the bedroll, called twice and heard a wincing grunt muffled in the swaddled blankets. (The voice, she had heard so little of it, but so much, the day before.

("Where is your home then?"

("Home? Boston, I guess, or someplace back there."

("Your parents still live there?"

("Parents? No, they starved to death in the potato famine before I was born.")

The bestubbled, stretching and scratching length of him unwrapped itself and came up on end. He looked around and blinked, and Marcel looked him over again and only for the second time that she had seen him standing upright, even now in the grimy stained underwear clinging in pressed wrinkles to the firm arches and swells of his young body. She would get it off him and give it a good scrubbing before the day was done, yes, before Og returned for his dinner at midday, if indeed he did return; a good and rare decision made by herself concerning a man, when it had usually been, almost always been in the tradition

169

of her way of life, the other way around with the man deciding what he would have done and with the means to pay for it; men, except rarely, were not to be known beyond the depth of their skin and their pockets, and that was to know each man as all men; to know a given man as himself could conceivably be rewarding if done carefully and wisely and not too often, and now, studying up and down the form opening to the morning, she began the knowing of this one: a runted child forcibly and prematurely weaned by circumstances that summed up the condition of the world as Marcel, too, knew it; child in the outsized body of a man that he didn't quite possess either, and so could be possessed, maybe as a chunk of jewelry not meant to be worn for outward display but laid away in a fancy-lined locking box for looking and touching in secret moments. . . . Body that the child within was more than ready to pass on as a gift or hurl as a weapon in an indulgent tantrum; lively child, savagely angry, no doubt thoroughly pleasing.

She fed him well. She tried to urge an extra cup of coffee on him but he resisted her in sullen silence, with slight motions of his morning-rumpled head as though fighting the alighting of a fly on his face or trying to break with a half-felt pain; finally, in what might have seemed an ugly savage mood, he pushed himself up from the table and, as he had the night before, walked out of the house. Marcel let him go but after the door was closed behind him tried to follow with a watch at the window; but he stayed out of sight of the cabin, leaving Marcel first to fret and feel the returning desolation, then to make herself busy heating water and washing dishes, realizing that he had probably only gone to look after his horse.

When he came back through the door she was ready for him: not coffee now, not food and not even a word;

she took him by the hand and half pulled him across the room to the bed and there, although his eyes remained averted, all the fury of the child burst over her and drenched her; her tired aging insides twisted as his senseless scattered energies funneled into her; then when her time was coming she looked for the face still turned away and saw only the eye of it — the eye that did not belong to this one but was sunk in the mine down in the side of the hill, that eye which had come to give her the only image of herself, and with sight of the image the ranting life ebbed out of her and slid backward from its high climb, this life that belonged to him with the breath ranting in his throat struggling on alone to his own solitary quiescence.

When Murphy was finished he rolled from her as any man would do, as all had ever done, and dropped into another well-fed slumber and Marcel lay old and awake and exposed under the crude wood of the ceiling. She hated the eye. She thought of running from it but knew without thinking further that she had neither the will nor the energy for running. She had drifted into it, but now she could see no drifting out again. The new smoke of piñon seeped from the lids of the stove, the smoke of today and the worn tobacco smoke of time past and her jumbled thoughts grew desperate and came to nothing — except move, go, hide, exert whatever power of motion she might have; and her mind fluttered around the room like an insect, resting on the table now bare of dishes and wiped, then the high shelf where her dishes tilted foolishly, finally on the floor creeping back toward the bed and board under which, she had figured, Og kept his money box, the tin box with probably a fortune inside and some papers Og valued, such as a marriage certificate which she would see and smile at opening the box in some other room to which she most certainly would drift. The box was big enough to hold the days gone and the days remaining, including, finally, the memory of the big firm body asleep beside her.

The thought of the box had seemed to enter her through an obscure channel, but now it had taken full possession. It held many answers. First of all there was Murphy, most recent of all her afterthoughts, who if he would not follow her most certainly would follow such an object as Og's box. There was also the sense of miles, the far traveling into an unknown and a rolling back of days to a time when life could have begun again and now would, to begin a new drifting of days; but the worst of it was, she knew that if she would make it become she would have to plan, and she had never planned.

Murphy awoke then, swallowed and sighed. He turned a sleepy frowning face to her and turned away. He needed her no more and knew it. What he didn't know, and what Marcel knew, smiling to herself, was that he would be needing her again and soon, for the child's needs are greater than the man's.

Sight of the openeyed Murphy returned her to present time and the thought that it must be getting on to noon, that Og might possibly come home to dinner, although the presence of a stranger in the house would, ironically, be the very thing to keep him away. But if he did chance to come in — and the thought struck with a charge — he would kill both of them and right here on this sagging makeshift bed with its loose slat. That would be the worst thing. If they left together he would follow them in his hunching one-eyed manner, silent and prying the thickest brush with the instinct of a hound, the quiet far-knowing sense of a cat and the dignity of neither, and he would kill as silently and surely as he hunted; but to kill them here before the leaving, that thought could not be tolerated. Marcel had no wish to preserve her own life, and she could sense no more of a life in Murphy than in herself, and as separate creatures it was no striking thought to consider their lying here and being beheaded like chickens after a brief scratching and ruffling in the pen; but what was the little weeded growth that had made itself felt in her in these moments, of which this young hulk beside her had some mysterious part, which demanded to be kept and let grow further, for a little while at least, which could be bought and kept and nurtured with the useless money in the tin box? Another day of being made dead was not for consideration: today she had reason enough to want to be alive, and probably she would feel the same tomorrow and the next day — except, something had to be done soon — except, a way had to be discovered, out of mind or out of someplace where ways were conceived; for no matter what else happened, Og would surely sense soon, would surely kill Murphy if things went along this way — except . . .

She looked again at Murphy who was staring vacantly and still frowning, looked beyond his head where the bedboards joined at the corner and she saw his gunbelt hanging. Of course, he had taken it off here at the side of the bed, as she had often seen such men do before, and hung it within his reach never to be quite forgotten even in moments that might pretend to be far from death; and also as was the way with such men as Murphy, she could not now recall a moment of the hours Murphy had been under this roof with her that he had permitted the gun to be more than an arm's reach from him, and Og . . .

Finally at ease, Marcel climbed over Murphy and smoothed herself down. She gently ordered Murphy to get up. Then she peered out the window and down the road and had another distressing moment, this time a deep sense of wrongdoing, strange to her and which she could not understand, until she remembered that this strange state she now found herself in with Og was the first time she had ever been married. The eye that she now surprised herself in the thought of extinguishing belonged to her own husband.

16

IN THE MORNING OG AWOKE as usual in the darkness
and turned his head out to the room. A lonely little
flame had sprung out someplace inside the dying stove
and was casting a fluttering square across the floor, and
a corner of reflected flame heaved and fell across the
bedroll that wrapped Murphy and reached out to the
sleeping head. Before Og's mind could finish the
thought, his eye had seen that during the night Murphy had moved his head off the pillow he always made
by wrapping the belt around his scabbarded gun.
Murphy lay deep-curled in sleep, his back to the room.

For many nights, perhaps a week of them, Murphy
had held this place on the floor, sleeping securely as a
child; and through the day the cabin had been his, for
he kept to it closely, never going outside, while Marcel
made the trips to the spring and the woodpile and to
the barn to tend the horses, including the piebald,
roman-nosed buckskin Murphy had ridden in on;
through the silent suppers sitting his chair brazenly
watching Og with two constant eyes while Marcel, it
seemed to Og, watched similarly from the other side
of the table. Through these days and these nights Og
had kept his silence, deep within it his waiting.

Now, on this day and before this sunrise, Murphy

lay hunched in sleep, his gun inches behind his head detached from him, a dead piece of bone and metal and no longer a part of the body; and with the gun separated from him the slow heaving form wrapped tightly in shabby blankets and stiffened tarp was all of Murphy. The gun lay there alone, five long silent steps across the floor as Og counted them, lay in its accidental spot as Og moved up on it, hand reaching. Now he was squatting beside Murphy and took a moment to listen behind him, back to the steady sighing breath of Marcel.

The gun slid easily, quickly and silently out of its scabbard, just as Murphy had meant that it should on a more appropriate occasion, and Og unbent. He withdrew as quietly as possible toward the bed, for his hand holding the gun had begun to tremble; he was afraid of it. If Murphy awoke Og might be forced to use the gun, and he had never fired one; the possible thought of it now was fearful. The voiced roar of dynamite had long ago come to be one of his pleasures, but never the sharp slapping spat of a gun. Shifting the gun cautiously from hand to hand he put on his shirt with the knife sheath sewn in and felt better; then he pulled on his pants and boots, got into his short coat and shoved the gun into his belt, loading-gate out as he had seen it done to keep it from falling through, and tried to forget for the few necessary moments that it was there.

The sturdy little flame in the stove finally gave out, jumped back into life briefly, then died apparently for good. Og listened again to the sleep breathing of the dark room; he could now see nothing either of Murphy or Marcel, and the good darkness folded around and cleared his head, soothed his nerves — the darkness now, and the day that would surely come, had always come out of miserly hours of counting coin in

176

silence. He slipped out the door, still with no change of breath, no stirring on either side of the room, closed the room behind him for the time being and crept around the mounded outcropping of rock that buttoned the flat where the cabin stood to the rising canyon wall — the rock he had seen often as he told, and retold in many versions, the story he had lived in preparation the past several days. Now he crouched behind the rock and raised his head slowly until he could see down into his own window, down where the cabin stood dark below in the fading starlight, the dawn a hardly noticeable glow among the trees on the ridge above, the window now a black hole of sleep and absurd sort of peace. Then Og stood up full, drew the gun from his belt and flung it spinning far into the brush where it landed with a mild whisper of twigs and leaves, no sound of its own.

Og then took the road to the mine and when he reached it a haze of light was just edging the slant eastern horizon. He felt into the rock crevice and got out his mine lamp, lit it and went inside to look over the fall from the final blasting of the day before, the lively bluegreen of the copper against the common earth-rib browns and blacks, all cut by the blast and fallen together as though there were no distinction — enough to anger a man, to have to pick apart the ore from all this garbage and make it be its own value, stack it with its own kind apart from the worthless; he hung the lantern high and began the mucking. He was mining deep now and drifting up under the ore pocket as he had somewhere learned long ago to do, even now hearing the voice describing the drift, yet a voice with no face and no name, only the knowledge Og needed; and each blast seemed to be bringing down richer ore and there was just no knowing how much there was or whether there was ever an end to it —

well, there was no end to dynamite either and no end
to Ogden Jenks, burrowing deeper and deeper away
from light and living. He piled the ore and squatted
over it and hefted the highgrade chunk by chunk in
his hands as he did every morning, knowing it inti-
mately, turning round and round the reality that this
was his — not something he had taken from some man
in wages or loot, nothing that had made him so humili-
ate himself, but taken nevertheless — from the earth.
Then with the great vitality that this small action always gave him he stood up and grabbed the shovel and
began the mucking again, turning up the damp smell
of rock and earth, the dark smells of not living and
never having lived which were Og's life.

Far out and up the slanting tunnel now showed a
dusting of light with the full coming of day, and not
quite an ordinary sort of day; the lamp glistened on
the humped and edged rock walls around and ahead,
solid now to stop a man abruptly from entering farther
into the earth; but another shot today and the wall
would be gone, emptied to join up with the tunnel,
longer path away from the sun.

He could spend the fury shortly in the soft globe of
lamplight that held his world, confine himself for a
time from the upper sunlight but not for too long; this
time in the deep hole spent with the rock and the ore
would know nothing of a day that was to be unlike
all others, this day which had been considered and
studied for many before it, now that it was here, must
be as much the common day as possible, must not be
gone too suddenly, its pleasures not abused — pleasures as new to Og as the late-coming of a woman under
his roof, and except for the woman Og would have
preferred again the grizzly bear to the man Murphy
— the grizzly bear which he could honor and respect
and kill, and which had taken his face from him and

set him apart from such ones as Murphy, the common brown rock. It was better this way, to work and let time pass and perhaps occasionally think of Murphy without a gun whose only thought now could be of running away, then the thought following: that the only possible way out of the canyon on horseback was past the mine, that the only possible way out was on a horse (even were Murphy foolish enough to try climbing through the steep rocks and clawing brush to the plateau above, he could not possibly survive long afoot). True enough, he might in desperation try to slip past the mouth of the mine and out of the canyon, and if he tried it he would probably succeed, with Og working deep down below and hearing no sounds on the surface. But Murphy had no way of knowing for certain that Og was down in the mine; indeed, he could not know that Og was not lurking at the moment within a few yards of the cabin. In any case, Og knew that Murphy could never gather the courage, even in the panic that was sure to be on him soon, to try making the run; and if Murphy ran away now he would only succeed in delaying for a matter of hours, perhaps a day, his eventual meeting with Og. No, it was better (indeed it was far pleasanter and more fitting) that Og remain down here in the mine for a while, and he picked up a piece of the highgrade and traced its color far back into a deep green countryside he had known, and not known, and disowned long ago, a place where a runted boy had lived and where people fattened in futility on rich ground and smiled and laughed and talked of little pleasures, their sounds in his ears and their books pressed into his hands.

Frozen in his memory was the sense, the longing to put it away from him, to put it all far behind him in the dust of his leaving; and in that time there had been a place to go, to remove himself — and to escape and find the vast privacy along the surface of the earth rather than by burrowing deep into it; there had been that place, told and retold, where the land was not soft and smooth and not nearly so gently green, land that would grow nothing on command, nothing except that which it had always grown and chosen to grow; a nearly empty land without rulers or rules or should or should-not or rewards for the like and punishments for the unlike but where wind and sun and storms punished unexpectedly and at will, justly or unjustly; a land that would not own or be owned, not love or be loved, would not fold soft arms around those creatures who lived on it and make demands of them; was careless of pain and death as a proper sort of god; a land that was all passion and could tolerate no passion but its own, no small sentiments of small towns and squared fields labeled with borrowed and ill-fitting names that in celebrating death advocated life; a place to go at that time for one who had heard a little talk and read a few words in a few books and had found that he chose to read without words, could bring himself to believe no talk and could discover nothing in himself that might be likened to the makers of talk, never made for him. Og, who had never led anybody and never followed . . . how was he to know that if he went there the green country would follow? How could he have known that a patch of the green country had grown into him and would sometime come alive to its own? He studied the ore and the humped darkened streaks, tracing smooth green hills. The stone grew as he stared at it until he slid out through his eye and into it, back into the green and blue time and felt the simple kindly warmth of those people, those who called themselves parents and grandparents, brothers and sisters, reaching soft hands toward him until he cringed and dodged and cowered and wondered why he despised their expressions of their feelings, doubted their truth, hated them as meek rabbits who ate grass and let their flesh be eaten.

Then the gentle countryside was bruised with yellow-green stormlight, flickering and weaving and wavering among clouds in black and dark gray sky and rain tried to come but couldn't and the clouded trees stood stiff and the dry grass waited; a vast loneliness settled over the closest hills with their fields and pastures and white houses, and no one and nothing was alive there any more, for the dry season had killed out and calling voices sounded weakly from beyond all lands, pleading to be found and led back and Og was finally alone in a dead country lit without sun. He shook his head sharply and looked around at the damp brown walls of the tunnel. The lamp overhead had begun to flicker, making shadows weave and bob and the supporting timbers mix their thick shapes with the slender handles of pick and shovel leaned against them, and the sharp shallow protrusions from the walls stretched long and snapped. He looked behind him and up toward the daylight haze, toward the mouth of the shaft, and he tossed the piece of ore back into the pile and walked with long climbing strides out of the tunnel and into the oblique daylight.

A thunderstorm had passed, leaving the rocks and trees soaked and smelling of themselves and tiny rivers still running down the steep side of the canyon and into little clear puddles on the path from the mine. Clouds tossed and fretted in the sky and far out over the rimrocks thunder passed away. Og heard a growl in his stomach and knew that it was close to noon. During the past days, with Murphy staying at the house, he had been bringing a small package of something to eat down to the mine with him. Today, with its unusual beginning, he had brought nothing. Suddenly it became important that he have something to eat, for it angered him that Murphy, who had taken from him, could even deprive him of food when his body called for it; then he remembered that he had brought food with him the day before, or on some one of the recent days, and had left some biscuits uneaten and put the package up in a rock niche inside the mine tunnel. It would be there now, if the small animals hadn't found and stolen it from him, and he went inside, felt in the rock and found the package. The biscuits were still there, and he angled one of them into his mouth and bit on it. The rock hardness hurt his teeth but a chunk chipped off and he chewed at it; then his stomach knotted, full of the meaning of the day, and would not receive the biscuit. He tried again, but being outside in the daylight, the trees dripping cold upon and around him, his thoughts were wandering up the road toward the cabin and that which would come. He could not eat; he could not have eaten the finest and hottest of meals and he could not eat the dry rock of biscuit that gave not even a stale taste. One by one he tossed the biscuits out into the air and watched them roll down the slope streaked with gravel from his mine and toward the creek just visible between the strands of brush that had grown up brown and deformed through the heaped rock rubble, the impoverished waste.

He sat down then on the brow of the bank just in front of the mine's mouth and waited for just so much more of the day to slide past; he was now actively depriving himself, sharpening the event that was to come and would probably be gone in an instant. Someplace above, the sun had bored a hole in the clouds and its sleeping warmth was reaching down to him through the heavy cover of cottonwood. If he could doze a while, so much the better, but he knew he could not. There were small jerking movements below his stare and he turned his eye down toward the creek where two chipmunks had found his thrown-away biscuits; their tiny teeth had already begun reducing the biscuits to crumbs that they would gobble to the last and whisk back into hiding.

Then a big narrow-eyed woodrat appeared between them from noplace and was slashing right and left until the chipmunks scurried squealing up a short piñon and the old gray rat hunkered alone and in comfort over a leisurely meal. His eye fixed on the rat and no thought in his mind, Og slowly slipped his knife from the sheath, palmed it and threw it, and the woodrat was pinned to the ground through the center of his body, squeaking out his anger and his life. Og's mouth cracked open in a laugh that had no sound.

He got up from his seat, walked over and withdrew the knife, wiped it in a clump of grass, and kicked the broken body of the woodrat down the slope. He went back and sat down, and after a few still moments the chipmunks darted out and went back to eating with an occasional brief spat between them. Og watched, saw their striped sides begin to bulge with the food that had been returned to them; saw their sleek fur and their tiny bright eyes that seemed ready to laugh. He thought of the gaunt gray woodrat.

Suddenly he was on his feet, and before a thought had crossed his mind his feet had taken him to creeping distance of the arched rock above the cabin.

1 7

ON THAT DARK MORNING Marcel awoke to a flame playing a pale game among old wood. Beside her the bed felt empty and she felt motion nearby. Then she understood that the gasping light above, which she had seen on other mornings, was cast by a weak flame in the stove through one of the slits in the firebox door and across the rafters on the ceiling, and she knew too that the same flame was casting itself across the floor, and that the movement she felt was that of Og someplace in the room. She closed her eyes again but they would not stay closed but sprang open, compelled to watch the rippling light across the ceiling while she followed the movements of Og through some sight other than her eyes. At the moment he was standing near the stove where he nearly always stood at this time of morning chewing on something Marcel supposed was cold sidemeat, chewing long with wet pasty sounds as though he were encouraging the juices of daytime to flow and awaken his body for the strange actions he carried on underground; then the death-rattle sounds from his throat as he swallowed big measures of coffee out of the pot from the night before and possibly a little warm from sitting out the night on the back of the stove. . . . Except that now she heard none of these sounds, only felt him standing there with Murphy's sleeping form wrapped in the bedroll somewhere near Og's feet; then she traced Og's body bending downward, squatting over Murphy in the bedroll. She could not turn her head to look with her eyes, to take that much a part in what she was afraid was going to happen; she could only remain staring upward at the flowing ceiling; waiting frozen for another movement from Og, another sound. It did not come. Long moments later she heard the door close, the room empty except for the sleeping Murphy.

Then, still not turning her head to look, she began to think: she knew, even without having seen exactly, that Og had bent over Murphy, but she could not guess what he might have done. She did not turn her head and she did not get out of bed because she could still feel Og, still feel a watching hovering nearby outside the cabin; after a while her whole body began to warm out of the stiff witless terror and she knew that Og had finally gone down the road to his mine.

The room had gone dark, the flame having given out in the stove, and she swung her legs out of the bed and stepped across the splintered wood toward the toothed row of red coals that remained of the fire in the stove. She squatted and her hand searched for Murphy, seeking anxiously, with some fear — of what she did not yet know; but before her hand could find the bedroll the flame darted an instant out of the stove and again crossed Murphy's cheek of soft stubble, his face sleeping closed-mouthed, and Marcel's relief was such that only after the flame had died she remembered again in the dark what she had seen. Quickly she reached out her hand and laid it over the empty gun scabbard, slid her fingers into the soft leather envelope and felt the slick, polished ridges where the cylinder had imprinted; and the day as she never imagined it

185

spread out before her. She remembered a time, and recalled her own amusement, when she had seen a short curved knife cut into the absurd he-ness of a grunting, groaning, retching little billygoat. . . . She was alone with what Og had left behind. She had even, in these last days, brought herself to think of taking some kind of action; now the time for that was gone. In the earliest moments of it Marcel felt relieved, for now the act had come, as it always had, from elsewhere.

Yet she still felt compelled to do something, even if it were only to wake Murphy and tell him, although she knew that with his gun gone Murphy would be something to contend with rather than something to rely upon. She took him by the shoulder, squeezed and shook and whispered out what she had to say, shook again and repeated it. Murphy stretched and straightened and yawned and groaned; then he came up out of the bedroll like a startled cat and was on his knees, his hand slapping the floor until it thumped on the belt and empty scabbard. A faint light was coming through the window and she saw him tall above her, his arm rising high and sweeping down; the buckle of the belt nicked her arm as he hurled the whole contraption to the floor with the rolling clatter of cartridges like teeth knocked from a mouth. Something between a whine and a growl was coming out of him, and he dove on his bedroll and wrestled it across the floor, now standing now rolling, until blankets and tarps fell in various inert heaps.

The shaped dawnlight strengthened over the room and Murphy began picking unwashed dishes off the table and hurling them flat and spinning against the wall, and their white wedges and slivers collected on the dark floor; then he overturned the table. Marcel stayed beside him trying to get a gentle hold on his arm, scolding softly. Next he leaped half the length of the room and onto the bed, clawing at the covers until he was tangled in them and struggling to free himself, gritting and groaning and seeming to curse but never actually making a word. Then the bed clothing burst apart and the room was again full of Murphy, this time his big hand sweeping the shelves, a can of oil upsetting over his head, and he turned from under it dripping and with a spin of his body he whipped the curtains off the window. In another sprint across the room he stepped on a cartridge; it rolled under his stockinged foot and he fell flat on his back. The cabin shook and Murphy howled.

From flat against the floor his body rolled into a ball and sprang up, still howling, hands crooked out and straight for Marcel. He held her by the throat but did not quite squeeze, and with his first real words of the day he called her a stinking old whore and a dirty old dryhole slut who had taken his gun away from him because she was sick of him now the way women of her kind always get sick of a man after a while and wanted that ugly old man to kill him because he, Young Murphy, was just too much of a good thing and she wanted to get back to that old used-up stud that couldn't show her up for what she was. Besides, she knew where the money was all the time and she had planned to steal it and slip off in her own sweet time and keep it all for herself, because she was a common thief, among other things. Marcel slipped out of his weak grip and planted her feet just out of his reach and with her arm and finger pointing straight she ordered him to sit down; his knees bent and his thick thighs settled on the edge of the bed and his face went down into his hands, a wide body shrinking in its underwear (which Marcel over the days had just never quite gotten off him for washing), huddled there as though the bloodless morning light chilled him, and with a long pained wail he was done. His shoulders heaved in big thrusts. "Took my gun away. Took my gun." His high whimper cut into Marcel's low tones. "Got my gun, he has. Stole it away from me." Marcel laid a hand on his bent head and worked her fingers through his coarse hair to the scalp gritted with dust from far places blown up by winds and gathered in solitary nights on the ground; she dropped to one knee beside him and hung her arms around the sobbing frame and laid her hand against him. She could have a good moment and in time he would be comforted (with or without her), even though it would not matter after the day finally shaped. It was good to feel Murphy's long sobs stretching out and dying away, with Marcel wondering whether there would be a little time or a long time. . . .

A long time, more likely. That would be Og's way; it was he who held the time. The steep rocks all around outside, remembered through the walls of the cabin, crowded in on her now. There was no way out except down the canyon, and in the canyon only the road past the mine was passable on horseback — no climbing the steep walls, no pushing through the brush unseen and unheard with a burden — for somehow she could not shake away the picture of herself leaving here carrying Murphy in her arms, even while she now felt the big body, fifty pounds her senior, give a final lurch against her.

Og would be back in his own time and it would happen, she thought, and she would let it happen, of course, and many other things and how could it be so different? For the moment she forgot Murphy pressing his head into her shoulder and let her resignation settle lazily over her. She could not believe that not-life was so different from life and she could not bring herself to fuss about it.

Day was full now. Outside, Marcel heard the same dawn breeze of all other days dying in the first sunlight and heard other gentle signs of morning: the sleepy senseless talk of birds and the highup whistle of a rock-chuck. Inside, daylight shone on the frozen turmoil, the piles and wads, twists and pieces, overturned furniture and the tools and effects of her unexplained daily living here in this rock-hemmed cabin above the unnamed creek. The layout of the room was a memory of one of the done-in ends of nights in other days — for instance, a payday during the building of the railroad when the saintly young Irish, remembering mothers, gathered at her place and spent themselves; and here, with her again in this unlikely place the same spending, the same loosing of energies and no more point to it than ever was, except to laugh and look and wait for the next to happen, just as now, waiting for both of them to be cut up here in this last untidiness of living, she and this pleasure-giving hulk that she, for reasons not important enough to know, had come to value apart for the moment, important only because there probably weren't going to be any more moments, this cradling body too large for her arms so cradled between her thighs as often as he pleased and often enough to please her, the moments of herself shut in and all creation, moments which she had heard tell of but never known in all her life of being wanted and being had while neither wanting nor having. She could be thankful that Murphy had no money or no notion of parting with whatever he might have, or he too might have tried to pay her.

She had moved up from the floor and was now sitting on the bed with her hands lying curled one atop the other in her lap; Murphy's head had come up out of his hands and he was staring with wide wet eyes. Marcel too stared as she let the sensations of memory cross over her while the two of them sat separately waiting. Marcel's eyes kept returning to a far little corner of the room which she had given over to the days before her coming to this cabin and had never touched, reminding herself occasionally that she would sometime look into, remake its clutter and perhaps clean it to resemble the rest of the house. Now as she stared into it her hand came up like a signal, finger pointing, and after a while Murphy's lost eyes turned and followed the direction of the pointing. There, poking casually up from behind the kegs and boxes filled variously with tenacious junk were the last inches of a rifle barrel, its magazine clinging to it.

Murphy was sapped by his orgy and for many moments he could only stare and register nothing; then all in an instant he leaped up and sprang into the corner and returned dragging the length of the thing out into the light, his eyes now full of a new animation examining it from end to dust-and-grease-caked end, neglect in every stain and streak of rust along the octagon barrel and receiver, dull gray stock. He ground the lever down with a wince and bared the tarnished copper of a stubby cartridge case; then he carried the rifle, long and heavy for a saddle carbine, across the room to the better light of the window, thrust his thumb into the breech and squinted down the barrel. He shook his head sadly, pained by such inhuman treatment of a firearm; then he lowered the stock to the floor and mumbled something to Marcel about boiling water, soap, rags and coaloil.

Marcel poked up and stoked the stove and put the kettle on, ripped up one of the curtains lying on the floor, and carrying out his further orders, found a length of string and tied a nail to it. There came another staring silence with Murphy watching at the window, sometimes glancing down and caressing the

190

abused weapon, while they waited for sounds of boiling from the kettle. At last Marcel brought the steaming kettle and Murphy began a series of small inspired actions, working as though restoring a life, standing the rifle first on its muzzle and pouring a jet of the boiling water down through the breech, dropping the nail down the barrel and drawing the piece of curtain on the string through; then he let his breath out as though he had just eliminated some diseased waste from his own body as he saw the plug of black corrosion dragged out of the muzzle. His face curled and, keeping his voice low as though he did not want to be overheard by some presence just outside the window, he let out a torrent of words about guns and fists and combat and allowing that the one thing in this world he couldn't abide was a knife, declaring the user of a knife the lowest form of man. He poured more water down the barrel, slopping it not quite so carefully, and he pulled another piece of Marcel's curtain through; then he squinted up the bore again. He was still smiling as he set the rifle down and poured more water through it, now giving a quiet talk on the care of guns and what powder and lead and priming could do to a barrel; he levered out the rest of the shells and examined them. He had his doubts, but one shot, the first one, would tell him how far out of true the rifle was, and there were more than enough shells here to do the job. If only the powder had not aged and separated to the point that it would no longer ignite . . . if only the rimfire primer . . . if . . . He took the can of coaloil from Marcel's hand and soaked the rust-frozen mechanism.

While Murphy worked, Marcel kept her anxious watch at the window, anxious now since the rifle had entered their lives. Once more she was seeing the road down toward the mine, still the road out of the canyon and one and the same time back into older days and out into new ones and a road with a man she could only half remember had passed down before dawn. She was watching for him, she guessed, and she had never watched for him before, here in one of those well-known moments of the old and new, the new here beside her working at cleaning a rifle. Just a little while ago she had expected to die and hadn't been able to work up much passion over it; now the rifle meant that there might be yet another day, which she would think about after a while. Just now Murphy was working the lever with loud rapid clicks that made no mark in the still clear air of aging morning outside where the old dust of wornout summer clung to the onetime green. Murphy seemed satisfied enough with the working of the lever and he turned to cleaning off the cartridges one by one and sliding them back into the magazine. Sometime or other he had quit talking.

At the end of it, he too, squatting and laying the rifle across his knee, turned to the window nakedly facing the canyon, dead and still and flat as a picture under a harsh blue sky with narrow seams of red cloud. It seemed that there could never be a movement out there, yet they crouched on either side of the frame peering out, tight with silence as though the occasional groaning of bent bones could sound far through the stillness. Murphy's eyes, sharp and blue as the near sky, covered the window; but Marcel looked and saw another eye from which she had never escaped and which therefore could not escape her, and the light of day was more fearful than morning dark.

Uglyman, uglyman — man with an eye to which she was lawfully and willingly wed; joined by a will out of childhood in a dim candle-starred chapel where crowned faces looked down over stone-still robes of faded gold and red, the light of flames putting life into staring features, by the wordless forceful law of whispered prayers, law that could be broken and remade but never destroyed and duty turned desire turned duty again and aiming the aimless. Here in the latter days she had no wisdom, still a vessel to be filled, emptied and refilled, still moved by changing airs and waters, the tilt and tip of ground she walked on, still confined by stone walls and trusting to the kindness within; first the old and never-quite-born child waiting for genuine birth, now the woman long past the summit years squatting at a window watching for her husband to come home along the road he took daily into his own life. Marcel could believe the emptiness she saw through the window for she felt it sightlessly — that Og was not out there and nowhere near the cabin yet. She saw the double path of road winding the easiest possible course up from where sight ended in the straight slope tufted with clinging scruboak, and tried to renew her feeling of only a moment ago that the road was a way out and into the open; now it was only a way in — the way for Og to make his return from the mine with the eye that held her image, the true image of herself as she had always been and always would be and never known that she was.

Murphy crouched there without moving, his underwear in taut wrinkles at the bend of the knees and the joining of legs to body — this fixed future formless as ever in other moments of change in her years, holding the old rifle in both hands now like a lance he was about to thrust through the window — at nothing at all, the vacant nothing of contrived childhood fears. (Could they both then be children? Could she, too, along with him, manage to be a child again and end the brief pleasurable thrust of imagination in the knowledge that it was, after all, just a game? She could not remember in her straitened childhood ever having played pirates, Indians, bandits. Had he?)

Something like an hour ground past; Marcel's eyes were drawn time and again to the mound of rock out there that had always shaded the cabin in the late afternoon, the early shadow of Og's returning home, a shadow that was still long hours away; for shadows were now shortening, not lengthening, in the hanging hot silence stirred all in a moment by the whapping flutter of a wing and the single squawk of a jay. Murphy cursed in a whisper; the sound had startled him. The silence set in again and even the slow summer stream became part of it and the long-ago breeze of dawn was far back in another season. The sun had stopped and the listening and watching turned to dry hot eyeballs and ringing ears.

Listening for minute sounds, they were startled to jumping by the one that came. In the first instant it was a familiar sound to Marcel — the mine blasts that shook and rattled through the house many times a day. But it continued, rolling down the canyon and up to the plateau above. In another moment the sky was no longer blue, the air no longer still. They unbent and looked at each other, and the flash lit their faces.

Could it be? Well, he was no natural man. He could come in lightning and thunder as well as silent footfalls, slapping once, twice, three times, then on a thousand running feet — as the rain falling on the roof. He could come as well in the fast fury of a summer storm as in the silent dry brightness of noonday. Why then did they take time from their watch, take their eyes from the window and loosen their muscles? Marcel gripped Murphy's arm. Keep watching; he'll come now, she tried to tell him. He'd come in the sounds of the storm, the rain blinding their window.

But he did not come. In minutes the brief mountain storm was ended. The air, freshened, relaxed to its former stillness, and the sun came out.

They resumed their positions. The slow drip of water timed another hour, perhaps; then Murphy whispered again. Marcel had seen too, as though a tiny circle of the crest of rock had loosened. Murphy unbent and let a knee down to the floor, moving the muzzle of the rifle an inch toward the glass.

Then the day made itself straight out in front of their faces. The head rose high above the brow of the rock, poised grandly as a snake — the face with the eye that seemed now to double, two great eyes that jumped out of the face and struck down on them with only the glass between (only now the glass was gone out of the window, vanished even before the sound of shattering); in another time and from another side of her face Marcel saw the forward motion of the rifle barrel, a stick thrust out in the hand of a child, breaking windows.

But the rest of the world, all of the world that could ever be for an old woman waiting outside the time of a child, hung in the savage eye out over the rock, the eye that had contained her, in which she had seen herself needed and thus needing. Uglyman, uglyman! — no! shooting would break the mirror, would destroy the circle that contained that which was surely her substance, herself that she had finally encountered and recognized. . . . No, no! — but the glass was gone and the flat, ugly day was inside and upon them. The window . . . but not the mirror; the mirror must not be broken, and Marcel felt herself being thrown on top of Murphy, knocking the old rifle away from the window (for Murphy was hardly there at all and had hardly ever been). But she had not moved; the eye had again fixed her and she sat stiff in her humble little squat, unable to look aside, to see what was happening in that small, casual place where Murphy performed his menial duties; she could only keep staring forward into the eye oncoming, closer . . . finally as close to her face as it had ever been, and she was looking, looking; a viscous silence without breath curled around herself and the eye, and then it was broken. The long-dead noonday was shattered as the glass with the repeating crackle, the slashing lever of the old Henry that Dot had left behind him in the cabin one snowy day far out of all memory.

18

THE SHERIFF AND HIS TWO DEPUTIES took a fast
reading — a simple surface reading, reasonable and
adequate. The sheriff, duly elected peace officer of the
broad empty county, into his middle years and going to
fat around the waist, kept a cigar in his square face and
put a match to it frequently; the first deputy, near
the age of the sheriff but pinched, wasting and going
to lean loose strings with bent shoulders, dangling
arms, and a large brown mustache that halved his
shriveled face and that he always seemed to be chewing, stayed a few steps behind the sheriff wherever he
went, in and out of the torn up cabin or the slapped
together open-end barn and corrals, up over the rise of
rock and down to the spring; and following the two
of them always at a respectful distance was the second
deputy, a newly-shaven boy who wore his revolver
with the self-consciousness with which he wore his
face.

They read from middle to front, end to middle,
mounded rock to desperately deranged cabin, corpse
to empty barn, copper cartridge cases to ripped floorboards. It was robbery all right, why else would anybody go to prying up a floor like that? Ripped and
split and stomped in, hardly a board from middle to

far end wasn't ax-chopped or crowbar-pried, enough to see under at least, over to there, that square print in the dirt under the floor, marks of worms and sow-bugs and centipedes in it, most likely where a box of some sort pressed for years. But then this business of the furniture: the broken dishes and heaped up blankets and such; now that was no doing of just the hacking and prying at the floor. No, somebody had done some fancy brawling for sure, threw dishes at each other and mauled blankets all over the floor and what all. Take a look at it, then look out there a good hundred feet from the cabin, the dead one, head just about blown off by the slugs grouped neatly in the middle of the neck and blood enough to prove he fell right here and never knew what hit him, head just tied on by half a muscle. Not a sign he'd been anywhere near the inside of the cabin and had any part in the ruckus, or even knew what was going on in there. And what did go on anyway? If he didn't know, how could anybody know? The dead one if he could talk probably couldn't tell the whole story any better than a man standing here right now reading sign — floor torn up hunting for the box, but no need to break up china-ware and throw spoons and forks and wrestle bed-clothes just to tear up a floor. No, bad business just to stand and stare around the cabin and let thinking get tangled up; better go out and take another look down along the creek.

Dot stood apart and looked toward the trees that he remembered colored by fall, bared by early winter. He had overheard the lawmen's conversation in Harris's store and had been drawn, first in curiosity and then in sympathy, into their quest. He had re-called his encounter with Young Murphy on the floor of the valley — remembered and had his hunch. He had led these lawmen here and for the moment he had no more answers — none that they needed to know or cared to hear.

These three had come in the first place into the valley, an uncommon place for lawmen, in search of Murphy who they said had killed an elderly couple named Davis who lived on a small but well run and prosperous ranch near town. These fine Christian people, as the sheriff called them, had married late in life and had one daughter whom they had raised to young womanhood in the best Christian way and who was a joy to their ripening years. This young Murphy had worked on their place, and after a while the couple found it would be best to send their daughter East. This had vexed Murphy and one day he tied them to chairs, seared them with a poker — probably to make them tell where they kept their money — then after taking everything of value he could fit into saddlebags, he shot each of them in the head, picked the best horse in their corrals and rode away. The old folks were dead there the better part of a week before a neighbor came in and found them and called the law. There was just no figuring it, until the daughter who had come for the funeral broke down in sobs one night at the home of some relatives where she was staying and told them all about Murphy. With her parents dead, it seemed that all she wanted in life was Murphy, and she went off looking for him and hadn't been seen since.

The sheriff went off too, properly enraged, and with the only two men in the whole enraged countryside he could find to accompany him he had ridden into the valley where lawmen seldom rode. They had spent some days among the closed lips and shifting eyes of the valley until Dot chanced upon them in the store one afternoon and they began the talk that had led up this canyon — eventually to this cabin and this corpse, just a marker sign along Murphy's way, as the sheriff saw it; for the killing of the ugly man was nothing to put a good sheriff on a cold trail . . . but the Davises, no finer people in the country; and here stood the sheriff looking at the story written so clearly on the ground he stood on that it was a pure insult — story written too clearly to be read . . . back into the barn and over the corrals again to verify that there had been horses, maybe three, here about three days ago and their blurred tracks, washed and pitted by at least three brief light sprinkles, leading out of the canyon, likely right past the sheriff's nose while he was wasting time poking around in the valley. Where? Which way and why? . . . A young devil like Murphy who could make his way and all too well with most any woman, respectable or not, and an old blister like Marcel Jones? The money, likely as not he'd have that by now. . . . And what would become of Marcel?

"She find her way all right," Dot said into the trees. "Ole bitch-dog wise to the swamp. Home somethin' you see when you young, smell when you old; and even us old dogs what got no natural home, we smell out one sometime."

The sheriff was directing his questions at the vanished money box as though it had never left its imprinted place in the earth under the floor — answering the questions himself, for the box was surely gone and its absence could only reveal that there had been a fair amount of money and what-not in it — a fair amount, for Og Jenks never put a dime in the bank that anybody ever heard tell of, and he wouldn't spend a nickel to see Christ — a man that shipped the kind of ore everyone knew he did. If those two ever got to the railroad with that sack of money in their hands . . . Best get to a telegraph station and send word up the line, because Marcel Jones would have to go a long way horseback to board a train at a station where somebody wouldn't recognize her, and likely as not she'd try to do just that, because Marcel was a lot of things, but she wasn't dumb; and Murphy would stay pretty close by her as long as she had all that money — that is, if Murphy didn't kill her for it, and no reason that he shouldn't do it because they could only hang him once; and if he did that the trail would be worse than cold with Murphy alone and unhampered and probably a good piece toward the Mexican border before anybody could turn around. Because, after all, it wasn't Marcel they really wanted in the end, and whatever Murphy did now they'd have his hide one way or another.

Dot was thinking his thoughts in half-spoken words as the sheriff talked on, each of the two men alone with his own monolog, while the other three stood staring. Dot was saying, "Don't matter none if you get or don't get Young Murphy. Ain't no more to Young Murphy than a jackrabbit eatin' a bale of hay just cause it's jackrabbit nature to eat hay. You takes a shot at that old rabbit cause you ain't about to let him have your hay, and all you got is a dead jackrabbit with a bale of hay inside him. . . .

"What Young Murphy do you all got a share in, cause he's all jackrabbit-folks melted up together like lead rifle balls in a pot. . . . Go on and chase Young Murphy; he the bad one and you the good ones chasin' after righteous-like, and his doin' and yours in the last judgment will all melt up and run together in the pot, and sometime Young Murphy get killed or die like everybody else — like a man not properly borned yet, and dyin' don't signify a man was ever alive.

"But this here dead one, Og Jenks, layin' on the ground, ugly head most shot off, he plenty alive one time and he live a lot. You can say his doin' was bad too, but you got to name it different. Og here, he don't never mix up rightly with the rest. . . . Ain't but one mistake anybody ever make with Og Jenks and that's thinkin' every egg in the shell got to hatch out somethin' like the rest of the flock, and worst for him was he make that mistake about hisself. He open a crack and the whole big world begin to trickle in on him, inside there where he all the time livin' hard; the world come in and make his bein' into doin' — what folks call good and bad tangled up together and can't tell one from the other. Then he don't figure his wantin' just right, and his wantin' don't figure amongst folks. . . . Now he done for, and he got hisself all to hisself, and that's all the world he ever want."

By this time all the lawmen, the sheriff with his rambling talk ended, had taken to staring at the corpse, listening with unconscious deference to Dot's quiet voice.

"So now you go on your way chasin' after Young Murphy and thinkin' on the things he done, and pretty soon most likely you forget what Young Murphy ever look like. You catch him or you don't, and the ole bitch-dog she smell her way home. But Og Jenks, face and man, you don't never forget."

The face — it was hardly decent to look on even now, any more than it had been in life for those who knew other faces by their own. But the lawmen's eyes became fixed to it, their own faces twisting into shapes remotely describing the one they stared at on the ground. Magpies, most likely, had plucked out the smaller of the eyes, the nearly useless one; but the huge one that took in all the world the birds in their chattering talk had passed up, and it still stared out of the sliced face as though surprised that it was no longer seeing.

If it wasn't decent to look at the face, it was hardly

so to leave such a thing lying on the surface of the earth where people must go on living. They would have to bury it. Seemed hardly enough just to pile such a thing with rocks.

"Me, I'm asmellin' too," Dot continued. "I know how it is with a ole bitch-dog because I been smellin' a long time. Weren't no place much to go any more except just wait around and smell. Never was much place to go, only when I was young just the goin' of it was good. Now, look like I done smelled my way out."

The sheriff and his two men had turned and were walking toward the barn again. Dot unsaddled and unbridled his mule and turned him into the corral, then went into the barn to see whether any grain was left, and the three lawmen went on searching — for something to dig a grave with, Dot heard one of them say.

"Now if you just wait here a bit I be back with what you're lookin' for," and he walked off down the wagon-rutted mine road. In a little while he returned with a shovel and pickax.

Soon the boyish deputy was clawing with the pick while the other shoveled away the loosened earth. The sheriff stood by, puffing his dead cigar, thumbs in his belt, as though anxious to shove the corpse out of the world with one booted foot as soon as the hole was big enough.

The pick struck rock with a grating whang.

Dot winced.

"I tell you it's all right if you use them tools a bit, but I don't want them bust up. They done last in my rememberin' this long time since I laid out coin for them in town, and I spect these here ones to last the short while till I can start workin' my mine again."